MAR 2 8 2001

The Samaritan

Nancy Rue

BETHANY HOUSE PUBLISHERS
MINNEAPOLIS, MINNESOTA 55438

A Focus on the Family book published by
Bethany House Publishers
A Ministry of Bethany Fellowship International
11400 Hampshire Avenue South
Minneapolis, Minnesota 55438
www.bethanyhouse.com

Printed in the United States of America by
Bethany Press International, Minneapolis, Minnesota 55438

Library of Congress Cataloging-in-Publication Data

Rue, Nancy N.
    The samaritan / Nancy Rue.
        p.   cm. — (Christian Heritage series, the Salem years ; 5)
    Summary: As tensions heighten in Salem Village in 1691, young Josiah
Hutchinson learns that he must rely on the assistance of family and friends as
he tries to help a beggar woman and her child.
    ISBN 1–56179–442–2
    1. Salem (Mass.)—History—Colonial period, 1600–1775—Juvenile fiction.
[1. Salem (Mass.)—History—Colonial period, 1600–1775—Fiction.
2. Puritans—Fiction. 3. Christian life—Fiction.] I. Title. II. Series: Rue,
Nancy N.   Christian heritage series, the Salem years ; bk. 5.
PZ7.R88515Sam   1996
[Fic]—dc20   95–25701
                                                                 CIP
                                                                  AC

00 01 02 03 04 05 / 15 14 13 12 11 10 9 8 7 6

For Mary Lois Rue,
who has the most forgiving heart I know

"Josiah, you be the bear!" Hope Hutchinson called out as she raced down Hathorne's Hill toward the Ipswich River.

"No!" her brother called back. "I'll not have you chasing me!"

"Come on, Josiah," said William Proctor. He stopped at the bottom of the hill and squinted up through the spring sun at his friend. "You sound just like a bear when you do it."

"It scares *me* to death," Sarah Proctor said.

Hope laughed as the girls joined their brothers by a poplar tree. "*Everything* scares you to death, Sarah."

Sarah's pale-blue eyes grew wide. "The way he grunts and shows his teeth—that doesn't scare you?"

"Nay!"

"Be the bear, Josiah," William pleaded.

Josiah Hutchinson flopped down under the poplar and stretched his 11-year-old frame on the dewy grass. Putting his hands behind his head—which was covered with sandy-colored, curly hair—he closed his eyes and smiled.

1

"He's going to make us wait," Hope said. "He always does that."

As the three of them sank down in the grass beside him, Josiah had to admit she was right. Even though there was very little freedom for children in Salem Village, Massachusetts, in 1691, Josiah liked to use a few minutes here and there just to tease them.

"Hurry up!" William said. "It's our first day out of school. By tomorrow Papa will realize it, and I'll be weedin' and hoein' and—"

Hope snorted. "Poor thing. It's too bad you can't lie in bed all day while the rest of us draw your water and chop your wood and wash your vegetables."

Sarah giggled. "Really, *sir*, a man of your position shouldn't be expected to slave as you do—"

"RAAAHHHHR!"

Sarah's eyes turned the size of pewter plates, and William and Hope scrambled up, squealing with delight.

"Bear!" Hope screamed.

She grabbed the panic-stricken Sarah by the arm and dragged her, shrieking, toward the river. William galloped after them, grinning back at Josiah, who loped behind, swinging his arms and roaring like a Massachusetts brown bear.

He treated them to another "RAAAHHHHR!" and stood up straight so he could throw his head back and impress them with the teeth-bared growl he'd been working on. When he brought his head down, all was quiet on the riverbank.

Of course. That was the best part of the Bear Hunt game. The others had found a good hiding place, and they would stay there planning a way to trap him—unless he could root them out first.

For a minute, he thought of Rachel and Ezekiel. They should be here, too, slopping through the delicious mud with their boots off, shinnying up maple trees and pelting the buds at each other. But they weren't part of the Merry Band anymore . . . and they didn't deserve to be.

Josiah shook his head and, still grunting and sniffing, scanned the riverbank with his eyes.

I'm supposed to be a bear, he told himself. And this bear had to find the hunters before they found him—or there would be no end to the teasing.

He stopped grunting for a minute and listened. The air was alive with the sounds of spring, as if the world were happy to be awake again. A couple of red-winged blackbirds were squawking. Two black ducks muttered to each other as they made their way down the Ipswich. All the leaves were swishing happily in the spring breeze. Only over there—at the willow— was it quiet. Unnaturally quiet.

The willow tree, with its sharp yellow-green shoots dipping to the ground, made a perfect shelter for hiding hunters. Right now, no birds were chattering on the branches and no squirrels were skittering at its edges, because there were three humans in there. Josiah grinned.

Still pretending to grumble with frustration, he gave the tree a wide berth as he inched toward the river. It would be easier to sneak up on them from the river side, because they wouldn't be expecting him. He'd had enough run-ins with the Putnam boys to appreciate when he had surprise on his side.

He stopped growling and crept slowly toward the bank,

still keeping his eyes on the too-still willow tree. Just a few more bear steps, and he'd slide around and dive right in under the branches that trailed the ground.

Trying to step on a grassy patch to stay out of the mud, Josiah made his final step. Like the top crust of a pie, the grass caved in, and he found himself in a muddy hole as deep as he was tall. He heard a chorus of hoots from the direction of the willow tree, and then three faces beamed down at him from above.

"Bear!" Hope cried. "We've caught a bear in our trap!"

"And it's an ugly one, too!" William said gleefully.

"We have to kill it!" Sarah said.

William licked his chops. "How shall we do it?"

"Death by mud!" Hope shouted and scooped up a handful of the sticky black stuff and held it menacingly above her shoulder, ready to hurl it at Josiah.

"Yes!" William said.

As the three of them gathered ammunition, Josiah stopped being a bear and jumped, grabbing on to the edge of the pit he'd fallen into. With one pull he was almost out. He tried to scramble to his feet, but Hope gave him a gentle push with her foot, and he fell back into the bottom of the pit, squarely on his backside.

"I didn't know bears were that clumsy," Hope chortled.

Josiah knew nothing made his 13-year-old sister happier than to have her little brother at her mercy.

He also knew he had to get up and out of there before they buried him completely. He made a leap for the top again and was about to hoist himself out, when in front of him, at the edge of the trees, a figure caught his eye. It was a form he would recognize anywhere: tall, lanky, and lurking like a thief.

"Stop!" Josiah hissed to his friends.

"Not a chance!" William said. "You're going to eat a mud pie, bear!"

"No, I mean it!" Josiah hissed again. "Putnams!"

It was a word that would stop the heart of any Hutchinson or Proctor. William's and Sarah's heads both jerked around, and the muddy cannonballs dropped from their hands.

"Get you gone, Sarah!" William whispered hoarsely to his sister. "Downriver. Hurry now!"

It took no coaxing to get Sarah to run from the Putnams. She was already scooting down the bank ahead of her brother like a terrified quail.

But Hope stared after them in bewilderment, and Josiah knew she hadn't heard his warning. A fever over a year ago had taken part of her hearing, so words whispered through carefully gritted teeth were lost to her.

Long, wiry Jonathon Putnam was charging down from the trees with his cousins Richard and Eleazer where they always were, right on his heels. All three of their big, red Putnam heads were pointed toward the Hutchinsons.

"Putnams!" Josiah shouted to Hope. *"Run!"*

This time she did hear, and she took off like a shot, up the bank and past the willow to Hathorne's Hill. Jonathon veered toward her, almost slipping on the mud himself, and Richard and Eleazer stopped and looked around like confused rabbits.

"This way, idiots!" Jonathon hollered.

With flailing arms and legs, they headed after Hope.

But Josiah wasn't worried. She had a head start, and she was faster and smarter than any of them. He stayed low in the pit and breathed a sigh of relief that they hadn't spotted him. He had been faced with their mean, beet-red faces too many times.

When it was quiet on the riverbank again, Josiah pulled himself out of the trap and looked down at the damages. His mother wasn't going to be happy about the condition of his clothes. Gentle Deborah Hutchinson rarely raised her voice to him. But that disappointed look she got on her face when she had come to expect so much from him—that made him want to hide his face in a feedbag.

He tried to scrape the worst of the mud from his shirt, but after two wipes he knew it was useless. The only thing to do was . . .

Josiah looked thoughtfully down at the river. One short dip would be just enough to get rid of the muck and get him past the kitchen door before his mother saw him. As warm as it was that day, the sun would have him dried before he even got to the farm.

Plopping down on the mud again, Josiah pulled off his boots and then padded carefully toward the water. The cold bit at his toes, but he sucked in his breath and plunged in up to his shoulders.

The sun sparkled playfully on the surface of the water as it swirled around him. With the Putnams gone and the mud falling away and the rest of the afternoon stretching lazily before him, Josiah felt peaceful, like he could shiver happily in this river forever.

It was harder than ever to find times like these now. A year ago if he'd slipped away for an afternoon, everyone would have shaken their heads and clicked their tongues the way grown-ups did and said, "What do you expect? He's naught but a brainless boy!"

But now—now that he'd shown them there was more to him than being tongue-tied and foolish—whenever there was something that needed doing, it was, "Have Josiah take care of that. He's a young man now, that one."

Josiah let his head bob in the water and watched a few clouds dance above him. It was good to be trusted and told he was nearly a man. But it meant someone was always looking for him now.

There was a rustling in the trees, and Josiah jerked his head out of the water.

Was that someone now, come to find him?

Was it the Putnams coming back?

He grew still and cocked his head to listen. The rustling grew to crashing as someone—or something—clambered toward him through the woods.

✦ ✦ ✦

Chapter Two

Josiah peered hard into the trees.

The Putnams wouldn't make that much racket if they wanted to sneak up on me, he thought.

And then he heard another noise—a grunt . . . and then a grumble . . . and then the panting of a thirsty animal. The crashing stopped, and so did Josiah's heart. There, between the branches of a thick oak, he saw the shiny brown coat of a Massachusetts bear.

Josiah couldn't move. Only his mind raced, reeling crazily around corners as he watched the bear thrust his gigantic paw inside the tree and bring it out again to shove it into his mouth. He grunted and bared his teeth at the taste of whatever he'd pulled out, then he jammed the mighty paw into the hole for more.

The bear was two heads taller than Josiah's broad-shouldered father, with claws longer than human fingers. The only thing that kept Josiah's heart from leaping into his throat was that the bear didn't see him.

Not yet.

Don't move, Josiah told himself. *Don't move, and he'll go away. Please, God, let him go away.*

But the bear had different plans. He kept digging at the bark and stuffing his mouth with invisible morsels. Through it all, he panted like a giant dog and grunted to himself as if he were annoyed that he had awakened, starving, from a winter-long sleep to a world that hadn't yet produced its summer crop of berries and fruit. Josiah sneaked a look down at his own healthy body, well-fed at his mother's table. He'd probably make a nice supper for an animal that hadn't eaten in four months.

He tried not to swallow hard for fear the bear would hear him. He couldn't feel his feet anymore, and he knew the numbness was creeping up his legs and leaving them for stumps. If the bear saw him now, he'd never be able to climb out of the water and run fast enough to escape.

Suddenly, the bear looked up from his pawful of appetizers and sniffed the air with a loud snort. Josiah felt his heart slam to a stop.

He smells something, he thought frantically. Immediately, he started to pray. *Oh, Lord, don't let it be me!*

Trying not to make a sound, he sank lower into the water. The bear's head remained still, and only his nostrils moved as he took in the scents around him.

Run upriver if he sees you, Josiah's panicked brain told him. *He won't be able to swim as fast that way. . . .*

But with one final resounding sniff, the bear shook his big head and turned his back. The trees crashed and the underbrush crackled as the bear slowly rambled into the woods.

Josiah didn't move for a long time—until he was sure the

water had shriveled his legs into nothing. Only when the trees stopped crashing in the distance did he slowly stand up and drag himself to the river's edge. He wanted to lie there in a heap and shake, but as soon as he could get his legs to move, he pulled his boots on and started to run—upriver and away from this spot.

He really wasn't sure where he was going, except that it wasn't home. Not yet. Not until he was dry and wouldn't have to explain all this to his parents. He'd just go—somewhere, *anywhere*—until he could dry out and get his heart to slow down again.

It wasn't until he'd taken to the road past Bare Hill and headed toward Blind Hole Meadow that Josiah realized where he was going to end up. The widow's cabin used to be the place to go for a warm fire and some words that would make everything all right again. Even after the widow had gone, he and the Merry Band had kept it that way, until they had given it to a beggar woman to use.

Josiah considered that as he trudged across the meadow with his clothes stuck to him like cold cobwebs. The beggar woman had probably left there after winter and gone on to find herself some food or money. Even if she were still there, she might not mind sharing her fire until he was dry. After all, the widow had wanted *him* to have the cabin.

It had been a long time since Josiah had even been near that little hut at the edge of the woods near Topsfield. As he came out of the trees, the memories swirled around him just as the river had, only they were warm thoughts—of the widow, with her little elfin face, and of the Merry Band, complete with Rachel and Ezekiel, with their great plans. It had been a special place where the most distant of dreams could come true.

Now a pitiful curl of gray smoke trailed forlornly from the chimney. Almost tiptoeing from the trees, Josiah crept carefully across the clearing. He reached one of the windows and used his already mud-stained sleeve to rub away the dirt. Raising his eyes only to sill level, he peered in.

His gaze swept the inside of the cabin, but all it uncovered was more dust. If someone was living there, they didn't have much of a life, as far as Josiah could see. There was no cup full of flowers on the table, no shawl draped lovingly over the back of a chair, no stew bubbling merrily in a pot over the fire.

Josiah craned to look more closely. Maybe he'd only imagined the smoke from the chimney. Maybe there really wasn't anyone living here. Perhaps he and the Merry Band could reclaim it.

But his thoughts were stopped short by the groping of a claw on his shoulder.

"What are ye about here, boy?" a voice squawked in his ear. "What business do ye have peekin' in my window?"

Josiah had seen the beggar woman only once, but he would have recognized her hawklike voice without even turning around. When he did look, a pair of faded eyes searched his face suspiciously from between panels of no-color hair.

"Well, what do ye want?" she squawked. "This be my place, y'know."

"Yes, ma'am," Josiah said. "I know, because it was my place first, and I gave it to you—my sister and I—"

A bony hand clawed the air. "Yer a liar! I took it from some wicked children who had no business bein' here in the first place."

But Josiah could see as she continued to glare at him that somewhere in her tired, hungry brain she remembered him. Now that he had a chance to see her up close, he realized she wasn't the old woman they had all taken her for. Although her chin jutted out nearly to meet her nose, she was probably no older than his own mother. The weary look around her mouth and the droop of her eyes only made her look ancient.

"So what are ye starin' at, ye foolish boy?" the beggar woman cried. "If ye've come to mock Deliverance Carrier, then get on with it. Otherwise, be off with ye."

"I've naught to mock you, ma'am."

"Then be off with ye. Be gone, I say!"

Josiah didn't have to be told twice. He darted past her like an escaping squirrel, and he was almost to the trees when he heard her call, "Wait, boy!"

He turned, but he kept walking backward.

She jutted her chin at him. "Have ye aught to eat?" she said.

He shook his head.

Her chin stayed proudly in the air, but Josiah didn't miss the sigh that rattled through her. "Be gone, then." she said.

He was just about to go when he saw something move behind her. Slowly, a tiny head appeared from behind the tattered gray skirt, and two eyes peeped into the sunlight. Josiah stared.

It was a little girl. She didn't have enough wispy no-color hair to be more than two years old, and from the way she clung to the rotting cloth of her mother's skirt, she looked as if she could barely walk.

"Dorcas, get ye back!" Deliverance Carrier barked at her. "He's not to be trusted!"

The little girl just stared at Josiah out of sad, hungry eyes that never seemed to blink.

"I can be trusted," Josiah said suddenly. "I'll bring you back some food."

Deliverance Carrier worked her chin for a minute before she tossed her stringy hair back and cried, "Bah! If yer only going to be mocking me, I want none of yer charity! Now, get ye gone!"

Josiah staggered backward a few steps and then sailed off into the woods, leaving the two of them behind, clinging to each other like they were the last things left on earth.

The Hutchinson house was nearly dark when Josiah got home, and so was his mood. He hoped his sister would have a hilarious story to tell of how she had escaped the clutches of the Putnam boys this afternoon. That would cheer him up.

But Hope wasn't in the kitchen where he'd expected to find her. His mother was.

"Josiah Hutchinson!" she said when she saw him. The heavy black pot she was carrying clattered to the stone floor of the fireplace as she turned and put her work-worn hands on her hips. Her usually soft black eyes were blazing. "Where have you been?"

"I—school got out—and I thought it would be all right to play—"

"All right for an hour, perhaps two, but not the whole afternoon!" Mama ran her hand over her cap, where tendrils of dark hair stubbornly popped out. "Old Israel Porter has taken sick—bad sick—and your father's runnin' between the sawmill and his house."

Josiah felt his eyes widening. Israel Porter—sick?

"He's needin' your help here on the farm," Mama said, "and neither of you children can see fit to come home. There's supper to be made and wood to be brought in for the fire. . . . "

"I'll do that, Mama," Josiah said quickly.

So much for being cheered up, he thought as he hurried out to the woodpile. Israel Porter taken with hard sickness. Old Israel was his father's partner in the sawmill he owned with the Porters. He was Ezekiel's grandfather and Papa's closest friend. Papa had often said that since his own father, Joseph Hutchinson Sr., had passed away many years ago, Israel Porter had been like a second father to him. He seldom made an important decision without consulting Israel first. He put great faith in the old man's wisdom.

To Josiah, Israel was just a white-haired man who didn't always seem quite real—but his hard sickness was obviously real.

And where was Hope? he grumbled to himself as he stacked wood for the supper fire into his arms. She should have been home hours ago, especially with the Putnams chasing her all the way. And even that wasn't likely. Hope had the mind of a fox. She'd have found an escape route before they ever got to the top of Hathorne's Hill. She was probably off looking for the first berries and laughing while he did all the work.

And then she was suddenly there behind him.

"Is Mama in the kitchen?" Hope asked over her shoulder as she streaked past him.

"Aye, and—"

"Tell her I'll be down directly."

"Hope! Where have you been? I had to do everything—"

"Shut it, Josiah, all right?" she said. In the last of the fading sunlight, she turned and looked at her brother with eyes that could be described only in one way: They were terrified.

And then she was gone, into the house and probably up the stairs to the room she shared with Josiah. He finished gathering the wood but his mind was far from fires or supper. There was almost nothing that brought fear into Hope Hutchinson's snapping black eyes or left her cherry-colored cheeks as pale as they'd just been.

Josiah hurried into the house to deliver Hope's message to his mother. But he wouldn't tell her that Hope was in a state of near-panic. There was one thing Hope and Josiah Hutchinson always did for each other: They kept each other's secrets.

But Josiah didn't expect Hope to keep her secret from *him*. Long after he and Hope had finished supper and the two of them had gone upstairs to bed, with Mama waiting up for Papa's return, Hope remained quiet. Josiah knew she wasn't sleeping inside her curtained bed, though, and he hissed to her through the darkness.

"Hope!"

"Go to sleep, Josiah."

"What happened today? Why were you so long coming home?"

There was only silence.

"Was it a bear?" he said.

The bed curtains whipped back, and Hope glared down

at her brother in his cot. "Are you daft, Josiah? That was just a foolish children's game. I won't be playing it anymore."

"I saw one."

Hope sighed, and some of the anger fizzled from her face. "You've grown up so much this past year, Josiah, but sometimes you're still such a child. Your imagination—"

"I did see one!"

"Good, then. I didn't. And there are more important things to worry about now anyway. We can't be runnin' about the village after bears, real or imagined. With Israel Porter dying—"

"Dying!"

"Yes," Hope said. "Good heavens, Josiah, the man's near to 70, and Mama says he can barely breathe now. That means the sawmill will be all Papa's responsibility, and the farm and this house will be ours and Mama's. There won't be time for games. There will only be time for being grown up, and you'd best get used to it." With that she yanked her curtains closed and shut Josiah out, alone in their dark, chilly room.

He stared at the curtains for a while, wishing she'd poke her head out and be a little girl again, full of sparkling eyes and big Merry Band plans. Something must have really frightened her on her way home today, Josiah decided. Something that had brought her out of their world of fantasies.

When he heard her crying softly behind the curtains, he knew he was right.

⸸ ⸸ ⸸

Chapter Three

Before dawn the next morning, Josiah was up bringing in wood for the breakfast fire, feeding the cows and horses, and poking around in the henhouse for eggs.

"Any bears last night?" he said to the chickens. "I know how you girls must feel now."

They clucked at him, and he clucked back. In spite of all the bad news yesterday had brought, his mind was happy this morning. Right after breakfast, the Hutchinson family would be piling into the wagon for their first trip to Salem Town since winter set in. They went whenever weather permitted, to worship there just a few blocks from the sea and the ships that Josiah loved more than anything. Maybe he'd have to work hard on the farm this spring, but at least he could see his ships on the Sabbath and dream about the time when he would become a ship's captain and take to the open ocean.

When he came into the kitchen to deliver the eggs to his mother, Papa was already sitting at the table, bent over his trencher of warm bread and milk. Josiah hadn't seen him since yesterday morning, but somehow he looked much older than he had the day before.

"Good morning, Papa," Josiah said. "Shall I hitch up the oxen?"

Papa looked up at him beneath his bushy, sand-colored eyebrows. His usually piercing blue eyes looked vague. "What for?" he said.

"To go to town—for church."

Papa shook his head and went back to his breakfast. "We'll be stayin' here for church today, and you'd best get yourself some nourishment. It won't be a pleasant time, I'll warrant you."

Josiah bit back the rest of the questions that waved their anxious hands in his head. Sinking into a chair next to the silent Hope, he started to eat.

A year ago, when Christ Church of Salem Village had first been allowed to have its own members and its own minister, free of the rule of the church in Salem Town, the Hutchinsons had gone to church one morning full of promise, for Mama and Papa had given their testaments that they had committed their lives to Christ, and they expected to be taken in as covenanted members.

But the members of the church had been made up of the Putnams and their friends. For reasons Josiah could never quite figure out, the Putnams had hated the Hutchinsons and the Proctors and the Porters since the earliest years of the village, so Mama and Papa had not been allowed to become members—to vote on the decisions of the church or take communion. They were expected to continue to help pay Reverend Parris's salary, of course, and to follow the orders of the church. But Papa had refused and had instead taken his family to church five miles away in Salem Town. That had brought much trouble on the Hutchinsons this year, but Papa had held fast. So why were they going back to the village church now?

Josiah looked up to find his father studying him.

"You don't remember, Josiah?" Papa said. "You were there that night when Joseph Putnam and I were discussing it. You even shook hands with us on it, did you not?"

Josiah's thoughts wound back to that winter night in the Hutchinsons' best room, when Papa had revealed that old Israel Porter wanted the Proctors, the Hutchinsons, and Joseph Putnam to join him in restoring the village church to God once and for all.

Joseph Putnam, who was the halfbrother of Thomas and the others, had refused. Papa had been unable to decide. He didn't want to go back to the village church, remembering how badly he had been treated. But he was tired of the divisions among the people in the village—and he and Joseph Putnam had shaken hands with Josiah, asking him to promise that he wouldn't let this happen in his generation. But as for Papa, he had told Joseph Putnam that night that he'd needed more time to know what was right.

The time must have come now.

"Israel has asked me to go since he can't be there to represent us himself," Papa said. "But the Putnams will surely resent our presence, and that goes for the sons as well as the fathers. There is to be no 'warring' among you boys, d'ya hear?"

"Aye, sir," Josiah said. That was something the Merry Band had already decided. They were going to do only good deeds from now on. He tried to catch Hope's eye, but she kept her head bent toward the trencher of food, which Josiah noticed she'd barely touched.

"Are you ill, Hope?" Mama said. Her dark eyes were soft with concern.

"Nay," Hope said. "I'm just not hunger'd."

"Again, I say we must eat hearty," Papa said. "I fear we've a hard day ahead."

As usual, Goodman Hutchinson was right. As the drummer tapped his drum to call everyone to Meeting, Josiah and his family filed up the walkway to the square, brown Meeting House. Deacon Edward Putnam was standing at the door, his eyes narrowed at them as if the Hutchinsons had come to church to steal all the members blind.

"What are you about here, Hutchinson?" Edward Putnam demanded when they reached the doorway.

"We've come to worship, just as you have, Putnam," Papa said calmly. "Now if you'll be good enough to get out of the way."

The deacon straightened his shoulders importantly and looked down at them out of his big, red face. Josiah wondered vaguely why the Putnam brothers—except for Joseph—all had such round, bulbous skulls. They reminded him of overgrown turnips.

"If you're here to make trouble, I warn you I will not hesitate to throw you out," Deacon Putnam said.

"There will be no need for that," Joseph Hutchinson said, his voice still quiet.

"It's the Lord's house, you know," Edward went on.

"I know," Papa said. "And I would like to enter it, if you don't mind."

It was obvious that the deacon did mind, terribly. But there was no more reason to stop them, so he sighed and stood back to let them pass.

Josiah made a point not to meet his eyes as he went by. In a few minutes, Deacon Putnam would be appearing in the loft where all the boys sat during church. It was his job to see that the young men stayed out of mischief during the long sermon, and Josiah wanted to remain as invisible as possible, lest Deacon Putnam grab him by the ear or smack him on the back of the head with his long tithing man's pole.

As Josiah scrambled up the steps to join the other boys, Papa took his place on one side of the Meeting House below and Mama sat on the other with Hope and the rest of the women. Josiah watched as Papa kept his head high and proud and took his seat beside Ezekiel's father, Benjamin, and Ezekiel's 20-year-old cousin, Giles. If anyone could come back to the church after a long, bitter absence, it was Joseph Hutchinson. There wasn't a better man in Salem Village, Josiah knew. He could feel his own chest puffing out as he looked around for a seat.

But after one sweeping glance, he deflated like a frog's throat. The boys' gallery was filled with Putnam boys—Jonathon, Richard, Eleazer, and Silas. All of Richard's little brothers were there, too, sucking their thumbs and squirming in their seats.

There was only one person there who wasn't a Putnam, and that was Ezekiel Porter. While the big-headed, red-faced cousins met Josiah's gaze with hostile stares, Ezekiel took one look at him and turned away. Josiah and Ezekiel had hardly spoken a word for months—ever since Ezekiel had fled while Josiah and William were being chased by two angry Putnam boys.

You still can't do the right thing and admit you were wrong, Josiah thought. Until Ezekiel did, Josiah would rather sit with the Putnams. Straightening his shoulders the way Papa did, Josiah marched to the front row of the gallery and squeezed in beside a straggly-haired little Putnam, who poked two fingers into his mouth and stared vacantly at Josiah as he sat on the hard bench. At his back, Josiah could feel the glares of the little boy's cousins and brothers, but he sat straight and pretended to be interested in what was going on below.

The service hadn't started yet, and most of the villagers were still filing in and bending their heads in prayer. Josiah saw Reverend Parris's wife slide into her pew at the front, and Josiah automatically looked for Abigail Williams. Abigail was Reverend Parris's orphan niece who lived with him, and she was as hateful to Hope as the Putnam boys were to Josiah. Even now, she curled her lip at Hope as she went by.

But Josiah's attention was nudged to someone else who followed closely behind Abigail. At first Josiah didn't recognize the wispy blonde girl who kept her head down and slid past Abigail to cling to Mrs. Parris. Josiah had seen her only once in Reverend Parris's kitchen, but now he was sure it was Betty Parris, the minister's 10-year-old daughter. The villagers rarely saw her, because, like her mother, she was reported to be sickly and especially in winter wasn't allowed out of the parsonage. Josiah could see why. She was paler than sheep's wool, and her arms looked like sticks even under the long sleeves of her dress.

With a jolt, as if they'd all been poked by some invisible tithing man's pole, the congregation stood up and Josiah with them as Reverend Parris made his way to the front of the church. The service was beginning.

There was a Psalm, led by Deacon Walcott, and then the people listened as Reverend Parris droned on in prayer. It had been a year since Josiah had heard him pray in church, and he hadn't missed it at all. The high-pitched whining voice sounded less like it was talking to God than that bear's had, grumbling on the bank of the river yesterday.

Josiah's mind wandered back to the bear as the prayers ended and the people were seated for the sermon. Deacon Walcott turned the hourglass. It would probably go on for a good two hours—plenty of time to reconsider the bear incident from all angles.

Josiah was reliving the moment when the beast had stopped to sniff the air when he felt a real sniffing in the vicinity of his neck. Trying not to jerk around and catch Deacon Putnam's attention, Josiah slanted a peek over his left shoulder. The faces of Jonathon and Richard Putnam were just a row behind him, staring too innocently down at Reverend Parris. They were up to something.

Josiah abandoned the bear memories and tried to focus on what the minister was saying. If it had anything to do with God, it was hard to tell. It sounded more like he was sentencing someone to death in a court of law.

"Like that outcast, misunderstood Samaritan," the reverend was shouting, "we are all called upon to shake off our selfish, sinful ways and help our neighbors. This man did not turn his head and cross to the other side of the road when he saw someone in need—nor should you!"

Reverend Parris gave one of the long, dramatic pauses he

was famous for, and Josiah filled it with thoughts of his own. The Good Samaritan. That was the story about the man who wouldn't allow a person who was beaten to die by the side of the road, even though he wasn't "one of them." Papa had read that story to them many times. Since he'd learned to read last summer in Salem Town, under Joseph Putnam's teaching, Josiah had even been allowed to read it aloud himself to the family. The story had always made him think of the widow, and now, to his own surprise, it made him think of Deliverance Carrier and her wispy little girl.

The hair on the back of Josiah's neck stood up suddenly, and this time he twitched around quickly, just in time to see Jonathon Putnam hurriedly sitting up. He'd been bent over, Josiah knew, probably to put something under Josiah's bench.

Pretending not to notice, Josiah let his eyes wander around the gallery for the whereabouts of Deacon Putnam. Josiah had spent almost 11 years sitting in boys' galleries in churches. He knew it wasn't hard to carry out even the most complicated scheme if you just kept your eye on the deacon.

Josiah almost chuckled when he found him. He was sitting in the upper corner of the gallery, supposedly to keep a sharp gaze on the sinful boys. His eyes were closed, and his heavy breathing rippled over his big white collar. He definitely wasn't interested in the Good Samaritan.

Josiah slowly leaned forward and looked under his bench. Staring back at him out of tiny black eyes was a puny, green garter snake.

You can do better than that, Jonathon Putnam, Josiah thought as he sat up straight. He liked snakes. He and Ezekiel always played with them, and he would have picked this one up and put it in his whistle pouch if he thought it wouldn't smother before Reverend Parris finished droning on.

He was just fixing his attention on the story again, when movement under his feet caught his eye. The snake obviously hadn't been in church before, because it very stupidly chose that moment to slither out from under the bench. At that same moment, the littlest Putnam boy beside him saw it, too. He yanked his fingers from his mouth, gasped, and stood straight up on the bench.

For a horrible moment, Josiah thought he was going to scream. But Richard Putnam grabbed him from behind and clapped a hand over his little brother's gaping mouth before he could get one out. Even the youngest child would be whipped soundly for making a disturbance in church, and Josiah wouldn't even wish that on a baby Putnam.

Youth didn't touch Deacon Putnam's heart, however. He jerked from his doze and marched silently down to the front of the gallery, pole waving and mouth pursed with disapproval.

"What is going on here?" he hissed.

"Someone let a snake go right in front of Andrew!" Richard hissed back to his uncle.

An entire row of eyes went to Josiah, and Deacon Putnam's with them. Josiah was a dead man, and he knew it. He wished he could slither away on the floor with the snake.

"It couldn't have been Josiah Hutchinson," another voice whispered hoarsely. All heads turned in surprise toward Ezekiel Porter. His big Porter eyes looked straight at the deacon. "I know him better than any of you," he said. "He's a complete sissy about snakes. I've seen him cry like a baby when he sees one on the path."

Almost all the Putnams seemed to like that thought, including the deacon. They all turned to sneer at Josiah—all except Jonathon, whose disappointment was obvious in the way he narrowed his eyes at Ezekiel.

"You'd best get the snake out of here, Deacon," Ezekiel whispered. "Or Josiah will become hysterical. I'm not sporting with you."

Pursing his lips again, Deacon Putnam stuck out his pole and lifted the poor snake off the floor and carried it down the steps and out the door. Below them, Reverend Parris complained on about the sinners all around him, never knowing there had been a real serpent right in his church.

Josiah didn't listen to him anymore. He could think only about Ezekiel Porter telling a lie to come to his rescue. He didn't dare risk a peek to meet his gaze, because he might get caught by the deacon. Maybe, just maybe, Ezekiel was ready to be friends again.

There were always two services on Sunday, and members of the church were required to attend both. A dinner hour was allowed in between, and Josiah and his family were on their way back to their farm, just across the road from the Meeting House, when Ezekiel's father, Benjamin Porter, hailed them. Handsome Giles stood beside him. It seemed strange not to see old Israel there, Josiah thought. Giles was always at his grandfather's elbow, both of them smiling at everyone with Porter charm. And yet it was as if Israel were there, since Giles was so much like him. To Josiah, there had always been something about Israel Porter that wasn't quite real. Perhaps it was the way he held his head up so proudly as he walked about, as if he were somehow better than the rest of the villagers. Giles did that, too.

"It's good to have you back with us, Joseph!" Goodman Porter said.

"You're the only one who thinks so, Benjamin," Papa said. Even as he spoke, Thomas Putnam's wife, Ann Sr., passed them with her brood and gave the Hutchinsons a look that would have shriveled an apple.

"Pay them no mind," Giles said. He smiled as if he had a great secret. "They won't be runnin' this church much longer."

"No one should be running the church," Papa said—a little fiercely, Josiah thought. "This church should be a union of brethren, not an arena where self-interested men can struggle for kingship!"

Benjamin Porter's face clouded. "That will be true eventually, Joseph. But we Porters are hoping that you are here to help us take over the leadership first, in order to give it back to the right people."

Josiah could almost see Papa tossing the words back and forth in his mind before he spoke them.

"I'll not behave as the Putnams do," he said finally.

Young Giles laughed and clapped his hand on Papa's shoulder. "We would never ask that of you, Joseph. Now, are you and your family going to join us at Ingersoll's for dinner?"

This time, Joseph Hutchinson's face did grow fierce. There was no mistaking the piercing glow in his hooded eyes that Josiah had seen there many times.

"The day Nathaniel Ingersoll—friend to the Putnams— was named a covenanted member of this church and I was not, I vowed never to darken the door of his Ordinary again, and I will keep my word on that. The Hutchinsons will go to their own home for dinner. Good day, then."

Goodman Hutchinson brushed past with his family trailing behind him. Josiah looked back to see Benjamin Porter shaking his head. Young Giles was still smiling.

"Deborah," Josiah heard his father mutter to Mama as he led his family briskly away. "I fear this whole idea may be a mistake."

"Do what you think best, Joseph," she said softly.

Papa walked ahead of them as they trudged through the mud toward home. Set apart from them that way, he looked lonely to Josiah. *But I suppose that's what being a man means,* he thought. *You have to do it all on your own. You can't really depend on anybody, not even the Porters.*

It was quiet in the Hutchinson house that evening after the second service. Mama sewed silently by the fire. Papa sat brooding near the window, instead of reading as he usually did after supper. And Hope just sat. She'd been so quiet lately. It was so deadly still that when the heavy knocker on the front door banged against the wood, Josiah jolted from his bench as if he'd been shot.

"You might as well get that," Papa said dryly. "You're up now."

Even though it was dark, Josiah recognized the tall figure with the oversized head as soon as he opened the door. Thomas Putnam didn't even ask if he could come in, but brushed brusquely past Josiah and said, "Where is your father?"

"In the kitchen," Josiah said faintly, though he might have saved his breath. Thomas was already halfway there.

"What brings you here?" Josiah heard his father bark. Thomas Putnam and Joseph Hutchinson had long ago stopped pretending to be polite to each other. If this visit went as usual, Thomas Putnam would end up being shouted out of the house within the half hour.

"I've come to find out why you've returned to the village church," Thomas said.

"Now that is an interesting question," Papa said, "considering how you've been telling me for the last year that it is my duty to return there and support Reverend Parris."

"But I know it was not at my bidding that you came back, Hutchinson. I want to know who has convinced you—"

"I don't think that is any of your affair—"

"I demand to know."

"God's!"

Thomas Putnam's mouth froze in midword, and slowly his eyes narrowed at Papa. "God's?"

"Aye." Papa narrowed his eyes back at Thomas. "That is how I make my decisions—by seeking God's counsel. Is that not how you make choices in your life, Thomas?"

"Why . . . why, of course . . . ," Thomas stammered.

"I don't know what's to come of my presence there," Joseph Hutchinson said more quietly. "I only know that for now that is where God wants me to be."

Thomas Putnam snorted. "Come now, Hutchinson," he said. "Do you expect me to believe that God has come to you and told you what it is He wants you to do?"

Papa sat in his chair and sighed. "No, Thomas, I don't expect you to believe that, because I daresay you have never had that experience."

"Now see here!" Thomas said. Josiah watched his big head grow crimson from the neck up. "You are insulting my religious standing!"

"As you are insulting mine, Thomas," Papa said quietly.

Too quietly. Josiah stole a look at Hope. He was sure she saw it coming, too—the explosion that always occurred whenever Thomas Putnam came into their house waving his arms and popping out insults.

But Hope wasn't steeling herself for the big bang with delicious expectation. She was curled up next to the fire, and her terrified eyes were wide and staring at Thomas Putnam.

"But perhaps," Papa was saying, "you don't understand my trust in God, because you seem to trust more in superstition."

"Superstition!"

"The crosses scratched on your cowbells, the horseshoes hanging over your doors. . . . "

"To keep evil spirits away!"

"Why do you not trust in the Lord to keep evil spirits away, Thomas?"

"We must do all we can in our fight, Joseph Hutchinson. God helps those who help themselves."

Papa leaned forward, looking hard at his visitor. "What is it that we are fighting that you haven't made up yourself, Putnam?"

"The devil, Hutchinson!"

It was Papa's turn to snort.

"Go on and mock me, sir," Thomas cried, "but I tell you, the signs that the devil is waiting to take over Salem Village are everywhere!"

"Where are they?"

"In the fires. The Indian wars. The locusts. The smallpox. The fact that my land will no longer produce enough food to support my family at our accustomed level of wealth."

"Your land can't support you because it's nothing but sharp hills and marshy little holes," Papa said, "and because you refuse to trade with Salem Town and make the best use of what you do produce."

"I'll not do business with those godless men!"

"Then you'll starve."

By now Thomas Putnam's overgrown head was the color of a giant strawberry and tending toward purple. Josiah was sure one of these nights it would blow apart right here in their kitchen.

"You are driving me away from my point, Hutchinson!"

"And what is your point?" Papa asked.

"All of this misery that we suffer is being caused by the devil, who wishes to drive us from New England!"

"This misery is part of living in a new and unknown land, Putnam."

"Nay. 'Tis a plot, contrived by the devil. The church is our only stand against him."

Papa leaned back thoughtfully. "Now, I must agree with you there, Thomas. As brethren of the church, we must make a stand against evil and sin and wickedness, yes."

Josiah could see that took Thomas Putnam by surprise. In fact, Josiah thought he almost looked disappointed.

"Well," Thomas said, inserting a cough and wiping his nose, "that is precisely what I came here to find out. What do you intend to do?"

"Just what the reverend instructed in his sermon today."

For a moment, Thomas Putnam's eyes grew wild. Josiah was pretty sure he'd heard less of the sermon than he himself had.

"You do remember this morning's sermon, don't you, Thomas?" Papa said playfully.

"Of course—"

"He spoke of the Good Samaritan. I intend simply to follow that example in my living this week."

Thomas Putnam looked at him blankly.

"You may have noticed that we have more than the usual number of beggars coming to our doors this spring," Papa went on.

That brought Thomas Putnam back to life. He gave a resounding grunt and nodded enthusiastically. "Aye, I have. Not a day goes by that my wife is not interrupted in her work by some filthy creature rapping at the door, asking for food."

"Well, when those 'filthy creatures' come to our door, we intend to give them what they ask for."

"Have you gone mad, Hutchinson?" Putnam shouted.

Here it comes, Josiah thought. *He's going to explode.*

"I think not," Papa said.

"Why, any one of those people might be carrying the smallpox. Or if you allow them to sleep on your property, they're likely to smoke in your barn and burn it down." His voice reached a shriek. "I tell you, Hutchinson, it's God's punishment on these strangers if they're poor. Good people should not be bothered with them."

"I see," said Papa. He leaned forward again, and Josiah held his breath. "Then I suppose it is also God's punishment that you have been cursed with land that will no longer produce—eh, Putnam?"

The explosion happened. Thomas Putnam roared like a thundercloud and stomped across the room toward the door.

"You mark my words, Hutchinson!" he screamed as he departed. "If you try one underhanded trick to overturn the leadership of that church, I will have your head in the stocks—and your land will belong to me!"

When the door had slammed behind him, Papa shook his head and chuckled softly. "That poor, confused man," he said.

"No, Papa!"

Josiah's head whipped toward Hope. She was standing up with her back to the fire, and the eyes that pleaded with her father were alive with fear.

"What in heaven's name—?" Papa said.

"Please, Papa," Hope said. "Pay attention to his threats. The Putnams are bad, bad people."

"Come now, girl," Papa started to say.

But before he could finish, Hope blurted out, "May I be excused, please?" and ran from the kitchen and up the stairs.

Joseph Hutchinson looked helplessly at his wife. "Has she gone mad?" he said.

Mama shook her head. "I think not. 'Tis just a silly season. She's becoming a young woman now. That's difficult."

Josiah didn't see what becoming a young woman had to do with it. Hope was suddenly frightened of all things Putnam, and for Hope, that was more than just a silly season. What's more, Josiah was pretty sure she wasn't going to tell him why.

✛ ✛ ✛

Chapter Four

The next morning, Josiah had finished his chores before dawn and was about to fill some buckets with seed when his father came into the barn.

"It's time those stumps were moved before you plow," he said. "You won't need that seed for a few days."

Josiah slowly set down the bucket. Before you plow, Papa had said. His father wasn't going to drive the oxen across the fields, digging up the rows while he walked behind dropping in seeds? His father was going to trust him to plow? Alone?

Papa pulled his jacket from a peg by the door and drove his big arms into the sleeves. As always, he seemed to read Josiah's mind.

"With old Israel sick, Benjamin will need to tend to the family farm business," he said. "I must spend most of my time at the sawmill. I'll not be plantin'. Young Giles will help you once you've got the fields cleared."

Josiah's heart sagged. Then he wasn't to be trusted to do the job by himself. And to be helped by Giles Porter—he with his flashing grin, smooth talk, and sneaky eyes.

"Have you some problem with that, Josiah?"

He looked up to see his father watching him curiously.

"Nay, sir," Josiah said quickly.

"Good, then. Hitch the oxen up after breakfast. We won't be planting so much this year, because our trade at the sawmill promises to support us almost entirely. But we must still have enough to feed ourselves, eh?"

That was for sure. Josiah noticed he was eating twice as much as he ever had, and he was still hungry most of the time. Later, as he wound a piece of heavy rope around a stump, he stopped to pull from his whistle pouch a thick piece of bread that he had slipped from the kitchen. He munched on it thoughtfully.

Hope had been quiet at the breakfast table again, and when he left that morning, she had her head bent over a big quilt she was making in the kitchen in the pattern of Job's Trouble. There was no way to find out what was going on in her mind. The only thing he was sure of was that it involved the Putnams.

Stuffing his mouth with the last of the bread, Josiah went toward the barn for one of the oxen. Several years ago, when he'd been very small, his father had chopped down a stand of trees so that they all fell in on each other. They had lain there all that summer, drying out, and in the fall his father had set fire to them and then carted away the embers. For the last few years, Josiah had helped drop the seeds between the stumps. Now the stumps were decayed enough to be easily pulled out by one of the oxen. That would leave more room for the planting of a nice field of grain.

It seems like a long time ago that I watched Papa chop

down those trees, Josiah thought. *And now here I am pulling out the stumps myself.*

He pulled his shoulders back as he reached the barn. His father was giving him responsibility, and he knew he was ready for it. But if Papa really trusted him, he'd let him do it all—by himself—without someone like Giles Porter around. Maybe if he proved himself by pulling out the stumps, his father would change his mind. After all, doing it alone, that's what seemed to make you a man. Joseph Hutchinson did it on his own—and he still had time to be a Good Samaritan.

Good Samaritan. Huh. It was funny how that story kept coming up—and how it made Josiah think of Goody Carrier every time—living up there in the widow's cabin with that little girl Dorcas, with probably less to eat than he had just wolfed down for a snack.

Guiltily, Josiah wiped the last of the crumbs from his mouth as he led the ox toward the field of stumps. Maybe he ought to sneak some food to Deliverance Carrier's and leave it on her doorstep. That was just the kind of thing the Merry Band said they wanted to do.

But that thought clouded his mind. Hope would probably have nothing to do with that now. It was definitely something Ezekiel would get his teeth into. But in spite of his rescue in church yesterday, Josiah still wasn't sure about him.

Sighing, he looped the rope around the ox's neck.

"What would you do if you were me?" he asked the animal.

The big beast looked at him blankly.

"That's what I thought," Josiah said.

There wasn't time to think about that once Josiah got to the field with the ox. His hands grew clammy as he tied the rope from the stump around the big animal and clicked his tongue to get the beast moving. What if the stump wouldn't budge from the ground? What if none of them moved and he had to face his father in failure at dinner?

But the broad-shouldered ox flicked his ears at Josiah's command and took a few lumbering steps forward. Almost like magic, the charred remains of the tree rose out of the mud and dragged along the ground as the animal kept walking.

"Whoa there!" Josiah cried gleefully. "You've done it! We've done it!"

The ox didn't share his excitement, but Josiah kept grinning as he pulled the rope from the stump and led him to the next one. This man stuff—this was easier than it looked.

Three more stumps came easily out of the dirt, and Josiah was planning how he would convince his father to send word to Giles Porter that he wouldn't be needed on the Hutchinson farm. He tightened the rope around a fifth stump. As he hurried toward the ox's head, he stumbled and almost fell headlong into the mud. A rock protruded from the ground next to his foot, still covered with wet dirt.

"Careful you don't trip, now," he said to the ox as he clicked his tongue and gave the rope a tug.

The ox moved forward, and then stepped back. The stump rocked in its place, but it didn't rise out of the ground.

"Come on now," Josiah said. "A sissy, are you?"

He urged the ox on, and again the animal strained and then stopped.

"Brainless beast!" Josiah said impatiently.

He stood directly in front of the ox's nose and grabbed the rope with both hands.

"Pull now! Ho!" he cried and, planting his feet in the dirt, he gave a tug at the rope. The ox took two steps and hesitated. Josiah yanked again. The animal ducked his wide head and pulled once more.

"Come on!" Josiah shouted.

The ox did, and the stump grumbled from the ground.

"Yes!" Josiah cried. He tried to hop aside, but in a slither of mud, his foot slipped. He was on his back under the ox.

"Whoa! Whoa there!" he called out.

But with another heave of his mighty shoulder, the ox moved on. With him came the stump.

Josiah rolled over and dug his fingers into the ground, trying to claw his way to the side. But the stump had come completely free, and the ox clomped ahead.

"No!" Josiah cried. He flung his face into the mud and threw his arms over the back of his head. With a sickening thud, the stump hit his legs and scraped up his back. By the time it hit his shoulders, the world went black and silent around him.

"He's coming around now, Joseph," someone said. "I told you this boy was a fighter."

"It's sure you're right, Giles," said another voice. "A child bounces back like a rabbit, eh?"

Josiah's eyes blinked open in confusion. Giles Porter? And Benjamin? Where was he?

But it was his father he saw as the fog cleared. He was bent over Josiah, searching his face, his cheek muscles pinched.

"Josiah, can you speak?" he said.

"Aye. Aye, sir," Josiah managed to say. He tried to sit up, but three strong pairs of hands and a searing pain in his back stopped him.

"You'll not be getting up on your own for a time, young one," Giles said crisply. "Shall I carry him, Joseph?"

Even in the pain that seemed to stab at him all over, Josiah felt the hair on his neck stiffen. Why was Giles Porter giving the orders?

"Aye, if you will," Papa said. "I'd best go for Dr. Griggs."

Josiah was about to protest, but Giles cut in again. "He's with Israel at present. What say you to my seeing to the boy while you men go back to the sawmill?" He flashed a smile at Josiah. "And then I can get to the rest of your stumps while you get yourself healed, eh?"

"I'd be grateful to you, Giles," Papa said. "Perhaps you can see what went wrong out there as well."

As Giles lifted him up, Josiah bit his lip, partly from pain and partly to hold back a protest. They were all talking about him as if he weren't there and couldn't give any information even if he were.

Maybe they were right, he thought miserably as Giles glided toward the house with Josiah in his arms. Maybe he was just the "boy" and the "child" and the "young one" they were talking about.

There was so much gasping and washing and poking and prodding from Mama and Hope that Josiah was glad when they finally went downstairs to the kitchen and Papa and Benjamin Porter returned to the sawmill. He was even happy to have Giles go to the field to finish the job, just to get him out of the room.

"That was a nasty accident, young one," Giles sang out before he left. "But you stay in bed a few days and you should be hearty enough to help me with the planting."

Help you! Josiah wanted to scream at him.

But he wouldn't have known what to say after that. Even now, lying there in the empty room, he had no reply for Giles. He wasn't ready for a man's responsibilities and that was that. All he'd done was make more work for everyone else.

As if to prove it, Hope appeared in the doorway with a rattling tray full of soup and cider. She sighed loudly as she set it on the floor by his cot.

"I'm not hunger'd," he mumbled.

"Then you're hurt worse than I thought," she said. "You'd never say those words unless you were well nigh dead."

"I'm not hurt so badly," he snapped back at her. "I don't know what all this fuss is about."

"'All this fuss' is about you nearly getting yourself killed by a stump. Seems you would have noticed it was wedged in with rocks."

"Rocks?"

"That's what Giles Porter said."

"A pox on Giles Porter!"

Hope looked up from the tray, and a smile twitched over her face. "Shall I pass that message on to him?"

"Nay." Josiah squinted his eyes shut. "I want to sleep now."

"All right, then," Hope said. "Call me when you've awakened. I'll send Giles up to check on you."

Josiah glared at her until she left.

Afternoon shadows had pulled themselves across the ceiling when Josiah awoke. He tried to stretch, but his arms rewarded him with angry pangs of pain. Carefully, slowly, he sat up and tested his back.

It hurt, there was no doubt about that, but he could still move. Cringing and gnawing at his lip, he went to the window and sank down on the blanket chest.

If you hadn't been thinking you were such a big man, such a proper farmer, he said to himself, *you could still be out there in the field helping Papa*. He hunched his shoulders and winced. Tomorrow he would be better, and he would plant the fields alone.

But the next morning, as soon as Josiah opened his eyes, he knew there would be no plowing by anyone that day. Rain was coming down in sheets against the side of the house.

He went stiffly downstairs to find the family gathered around the table for breakfast, and as he sank into his chair, he noticed, guiltily, that Hope's hair was damp from being out doing his chores.

"Why are you out of bed, Josiah?" Mama asked.

"I'm fine," Josiah said.

"Aye, is that why you're sitting up as if you had a poker for a backbone?" Papa said.

"There's work to be done," Josiah said.

Papa surveyed him for a moment with eyes that went into Josiah like beams of light.

"'Twas an accident," Papa said. "It could have happened to anyone."

Not to you, Josiah thought miserably.

"Take another day to rest," Papa said. "It's raining as it is, and you'll be no good to us until you're healed, eh?"

It wasn't really a question, but Josiah said, "Aye, sir."

After Papa left for the sawmill and Mama and Hope went upstairs to clean, Josiah went restlessly to the window and looked at the rain. At least he didn't have to watch Giles doing his work today. But what else was there to do? How often he'd longed for time all to himself. Now that he had it, he couldn't stand himself.

Do something, Josiah, he thought. *Get your mind off of yourself.*

Mysteriously, his next thought was of Deliverance Carrier. *Was she standing at the window, looking out and wondering what to do next, just to survive?*

Josiah looked over his shoulder at the leftover breakfast food that stood on the shelves, carefully covered with napkins. His head still ached, but it managed to put together the beginnings of a plan.

He slipped to the shelf and pulled down a rough, cloth napkin, a half a loaf of day-old bread, and a hunk of beef jerky. As soon as he got the food wrapped up, he could take off for the widow's cabin and—

"Josiah Hutchinson, what are you doing?"

Josiah jerked his head up and stared at Hope.

"Packing a picnic," he said quickly. "Papa said there would be no planting today—"

Her black eyebrows shot up. "A picnic in the rain. How lovely."

"Want to come?" Josiah said hopefully.

But even as he watched her, Hope's face clouded over like the sky overhead, and she shook her head. "Unlike you, I have work to do," she said. She turned her back to him to poke at the fire, but she straightened suddenly. "Whatever it is you're doing with that food, Josiah, just stay out of trouble," she said.

Josiah shook his head. "There will be no trouble."

"You can never be sure," she said.

Although Josiah turned down the brim of his hat, he could barely see through the rain as he trudged across Thorndike, Davenport, and Solomon's Hills toward Topsfield, cringing with every throb that went through him. He was soaked to the skin by the time he reached the widow's cabin.

At least Deliverance won't be lurking in the yard, Josiah thought as he crept from the trees with the parcel of food still tucked under his coat.

But just as he placed the bulky napkin on the stoop and reached up to knock on the door, Deliverance herself squawked from the direction of the abandoned vegetable garden.

"What are ye about here?" she screeched as she sloshed toward him, waving a muddy trowel. "I told ye this is *my* property now!"

"I've brought you something to eat," he said, pointing to the small bundle.

They both looked at it now. It was turning into a pathetic clump in the rain.

"That's food?" she said.

"Aye, but you'd best get it in out of the wet—"

"Ye mocked me before, and now you've brought yer family's garbage!" she cried. And with one mighty swish of her gardening shovel, she smacked the parcel from the step and across the yard. Josiah watched as the napkin burst open and the bread and jerky turned into mush before his eyes.

"You had naught to do that!" he cried. "You said you were hungry. I only thought to help!"

"'Thought to help' my left foot!" she shouted back. "You only thought to taunt me. Now be off with ye!"

She got her trowel halfway into a heave before Josiah turned and went toward the trees.

He plastered himself behind a slippery trunk and peered back into the rain. She had her back to him already, and she was limping away. Josiah stared.

She was heading right for the parcel of food.

Josiah watched as she picked it up. Standing there with the cold rain pelting her, she stuffed a soggy piece of bread into her mouth and closed her eyes. Quickly, Josiah turned away.

He had trudged only a few steps when he thought he heard a gentle rustling behind him. The word *bear* formed in his mind like an engraving, and he froze on the path.

Nothing. No sound, except maybe one wet leaf sliding against another. Surely not enough to be a bear.

Holding his breath, Josiah turned around.

"A-a-a-h!" he shouted. And then he caught his breath. Standing two steps away was Dorcas Carrier.

She was as startled by his cry as he was to find her there, and her two elflike hands came up over her eyes.

"It's all right," Josiah said quickly. "I won't hurt you. It's just—you frightened me."

Now that's a brave lad, he told himself as she peeked at him through her fingers.

He squatted carefully and peered into her little face, which could barely be seen, what with her hands covering her eyes and her wet, wispy hair covering the rest.

"What are you doing out here?" he said.

He wasn't surprised that she didn't answer.

"Go on home to your mother now," he said, "before she—"

He didn't finish the sentence. Who could tell what *that* mother would do to a child who had wandered off?

"Go on now," he said again. "Your mother will be looking for you."

But instead of turning and running back toward the cabin, Dorcas Carrier pulled her hands away from her eyes and curled one of them around his fingers.

"What are you doing?" Josiah said. "Just run home! That way!" He tried to pull his hand away to point, but she clung to it like a stubborn cobweb to a corner.

What on earth? Josiah thought. He couldn't have felt more ridiculous, standing in the rain with a two-year-old hanging from his palm, than if he'd run from his house in his underdrawers.

"What do you want?" he said desperately.

She tilted her pixielike head back to look at him, and then pointed straight at the cabin. Just as she did, Josiah heard a voice coming from the same direction. "Dorcas!" it shrieked.

"You want *me* to take you back?" Josiah said. She nodded.

I'd rather walk straight into our fireplace with the supper fire blazing, he wanted to say to her. But the screeching coming from the cabin yard grew shriller and louder, and the little hand that curled around his fingers squeezed tighter.

"All right, then," he said.

He took off toward the cabin with Dorcas in tow, but they didn't go two steps before her fairy-feet flew out from under her and she was flopping at the end of his hand like a minnow on a hook.

"Dorcas! Dorcas, where are ye?" came the frantic cawing from the yard.

Josiah reached down and caught little Dorcas up in his arms. "Hold on," he said grimly. And together they went toward the cabin.

"She's here!" Josiah called out as he emerged from the trees.

Deliverance screeched to a halt a few steps away and made for him like an angry bull.

"She followed me!" Josiah cried—and he held Dorcas straight out in front of him with both hands, so her feet dangled from beneath her skirts like a rag doll's.

Deliverance Carrier probably would have gone after his cheeks with her fingernails, if Dorcas hadn't turned her face around and looked straight into Josiah's eyes and smiled.

Even as thin as her cheeks were, dimples appeared faintly in each one, and the pale-blue eyes almost took on a shine.

Josiah looked at Deliverance. Both her hands had dropped to her sides and all the anger drained from her face.

"Let me have her," she said in a dull voice.

Gladly, Josiah thought. He put Dorcas straight into her mother's arms, but as he did, the little girl put up a squall that would have put a newborn calf to shame.

"What are ye caterwaulin' about?" Deliverance scolded her. Josiah could feel his face turning as red as a Putnam's. Little Dorcas Carrier was kicking her feet and stretching out her arms straight for him.

She wants me to take her, he thought in a panic.

"I must go home now!" he said to Deliverance. And before she could answer, he was back into the trees and heading for Salem Village. He could hear Dorcas screaming until he was well across Blind Hole Meadow.

When he was in too much pain to run anymore, Josiah slowed to a walk. So much for being a Good Samaritan.

But even as he returned to his house, Josiah couldn't get Deliverance Carrier out of his head. It would be easy to forget about helping a grouchy woman who came after you with a gardening trowel, if that were all there was to her. But there was something about her that he couldn't push aside so easily.

As he reached the corner of the kitchen, Josiah looked up, and his eye was caught by a face in the window. It was Hope, and she didn't see her brother as she gazed beyond him, beyond the farmyard, beyond everything, Josiah was sure.

There was something different about her face—a look she'd never worn before. But it was also a look he'd seen somewhere else today—on Deliverance Carrier.

He still didn't know what it was exactly. But now he knew what it wasn't. It was a look that didn't have a drop of hope in it.

✣ ✦ ✣

Chapter Five

After two days of impatiently resting and watching the rain, Josiah finally awoke to a day with sunshine in the sky and no pain in his muscles. He was sure he'd be plowing today, and it was time to convince his father that he could do it alone.

But before he had a chance, Papa made an announcement at the breakfast table.

"Deborah," Papa said between spoonfuls of corn bread, "'tis time for beating the bounds."

"Aye," Goody Hutchinson answered as she refilled her husband's pewter mug with milk.

"'Tis especially important this year after all the squabbling over boundaries last winter. Josiah, what say you to coming with me?"

Josiah froze with his spoon in midair, dripping maple syrup onto the table. "I, sir?" he said.

"I see no other Josiah in the room."

"Josiah, your spoon," Mama said softly.

Josiah lowered his dripping spoon and stole a look at Hope. He expected her to be rolling her eyes in disgust at the mess he was making, or glaring with envy that he was about to embark on an adventure that was denied to her because she was a girl. But she was toying with her uneaten breakfast with the tip of her spoon.

"You have no interest in going, then?" Papa said.

"Oh, no, I mean, aye!"

"Be sure your chores are done by noonday, then. You have some catching up to do. We shall leave directly after dinner."

"Aye, sir," Josiah said, clearly this time.

To be included in "beating the bounds" was something Josiah had been waiting for since he had been old enough to see out the window as his father set off on foot in the spring to make known the boundaries of his vast property. It was a custom all the men in Massachusetts villages participated in, and those who had sons old enough took them along. The idea was to keep fresh in their minds the boundaries and division lines of their fathers' properties—so when those lands became their own, they would have a sharp memory of walking them year after year.

Josiah wasn't sure why the outing was called *beating* the bounds, and he didn't care as he hurried through his chores that day. All he could think about was that he had jumped across another creek in his life. Having Papa decide that he was now old enough to understand the importance of all that they owned, that was like being told you were nearly a man. Maybe he could change Papa's mind about the plowing after all.

He was out by the woodshed, picking up a small pile of

wood because his back was still sore, when he heard someone whispering his name.

"Who's there?" he said.

There was only another hoarse whisper. "Josiah."

"Who's there?" he said, louder this time.

Hope's cap, fringed with dark curls, appeared from the brush, and she beckoned him closer.

"What on earth?" he said as he joined her in the bushes.

"Just listen to me," she said. Her eyes were dark and serious.

"Why are we whispering?"

"Because you never know who's lurking about," she said. Josiah started to laugh, but he caught the chuckle in his throat as she cast frightened glances over her shoulders.

"All right, then," she said. "You're to go perambulating this afternoon with Papa, aye?"

"Aye." *Perambulating* was the proper name for beating the bounds, he remembered. Hope *would* know that. Even without the schooling he had, she always seemed to be smarter.

"Then you must be careful out there," she said. "You must promise me that you will never leave Papa's side, not for a moment."

"Why?" he said, his face crinkling.

"Because all the men from every family will be out there— with their sons."

"I know that, but—"

"Must I draw you a picture of everything, Josiah?" she said. Her voice was laced with panic.

"Perhaps you should, because I don't know what you're talking about," Josiah said.

"Putnams," she said.

"Don't be a ninny, Hope," Josiah said, and this time he didn't stop the laughter that bubbled up in his throat. "I'm not stupid. I'm always on the lookout for those mongrels—"

"You don't understand!" she cried. She clutched at his arm. "They are much more dangerous than we ever dreamed, Josiah."

Josiah could feel her trembling through his shirtsleeve.

"Why are you so scared of them all of a sudden?" he said. "You were always so brave when it came to the Putnams."

"I was always so stupid, and so were you!" She sobbed it more than said it, and before Josiah could ask her another question, she had bunched her long skirts up into her arms and darted toward the house. She left behind her a haunting chant in Josiah's brain: *They are much more dangerous than we ever dreamed.*

But it was hard to keep even that mysterious thought in his mind as he and Papa set out to beat the bounds that afternoon. He didn't even notice that it was a delicious day, with the fruit trees all in blossom and the air soft and warm with the promise of summer. He just tried to remember what it was like walking beside his father, matching his long, firm strides as they set out to the south end of the Hutchinson property. He wanted to be able to recall it all later.

To his surprise, his father stopped him under the willow tree at the southeast corner of their farm and, with his knife, set about cutting off a thin branch.

"When my father was a boy in England," Papa said as he whittled, "boys were not so excited at the prospect of walking their land as you are. Their properties were somewhat larger, and it probably took them the better part of a day."

Josiah nodded as his father pulled off the branch and reached inside his jacket to pull out what looked to Josiah to be several strands of woolen yarn about eight inches long, braided together and fastened with a bit of wood.

"So to induce the boys to go with their fathers on these walks," Papa went on, "they were given a gift. I have decided to keep up that tradition with you, Josiah."

He put the strange wand with its little points into Josiah's hand. Josiah tried not to frown as he looked at it. His mind was racing. Was he supposed to know what this was? Should he risk appearing to be a complete idiot by asking?

Finally, he looked quizzically at his father. The rare faint twitching of a smile was playing at the corners of Papa's mouth.

"I'm certain you'll put that to good use," he said.

"Aye, sir," Josiah said. He cleared his throat. "But for what?"

For the first time in many weeks, Josiah heard his father chuckle. "There is no shame in asking an honest question," he said. "How would you know that in my father's day, these points were used to tie the hose to the knees of the breeches."

"Hose!" Josiah cried. The men in Salem Village wore thick woolen stockings with their breeches, and they were lucky to have time to give them a firm yank with their hands before they stuffed their feet into their boots and went to work.

"Or the waistband of the breeches to the jacket," Papa continued.

Josiah snorted, and Papa chuckled again. "It's a meaningless custom now, although we can use it as it was originally used in perambulating if you wish."

Josiah's eyebrows knotted together.

"At the most important boundaries, the boys were smartly whipped with their wands to impress the bounds upon their memories. Thus the term *beating the bounds.*" His blue eyes twinkled. "We can be true to tradition if you like."

Josiah quickly shook his head. "I'd rather think of it as a meaningless custom, sir."

For a minute, Papa's face softened, and his hand passed quickly over Josiah's shoulder. And then just as quickly the lines reappeared in his face, and he looked toward the west. "The work we have ahead of us is not meaningless. The stiff-necked people in this village will take your land right out from under you if you're not certain what you own. Come, then, let us be certain."

So for the next hour, Josiah carried his funny little set of points and followed his father along the edges of the tiny farms that belonged to the Houltons and the Haineses and the Ingersolls, then northeast across the road, past the Meeting House to the base of Thorndike Hill. This was the Blessing Place his father had brought him to a long time ago. It was where his grandfather had blessed their land when he'd first come to Salem Village. It looked anything but blessed now, after the fire that had been set there last winter. Josiah tried to shake off the sad memories as he and Papa looked down on the Meeting House.

"You know the land the church sits on once belonged to the Hutchinsons," Papa said. "Your grandfather donated it to the parish for the building of a Meeting House." His voice grew grave. "My father was moved by the Lord to give the land. I pray someday that gift will bear good fruit."

Josiah nodded and followed his father on.

Not only did Papa make sure Josiah knew where the Hutchinsons' property was, but what land belonged to the Putnams as well. "They will shoot you down if you step onto their property uninvited," Goodman Hutchinson said, pointing to a swampy piece of property belonging to Nathaniel Putnam. "Though why they would worry about it is a mystery to me. Most of it is unfit for farming anyway."

Still shaking his head, he led Josiah over Hadlock's Bridge and toward the Ipswich Road. "This is not our property here, but we must cross these lands to reach the rest of our ownings around the sawmill."

They walked along in a silence that was comfortable to Josiah. It was good to be walking beside his father, matching his strides, sharing his thoughts.

Perhaps now was a good time to bring up the subject.

"Papa—" he said. He knew his voice was faltering, and he cleared his throat. "I think, perhaps, I can handle the plowing—alone."

"Alone?"

"Aye. Without Giles Porter."

"Do you now?" Papa said. He didn't stop walking, but his voice was sharp, and Josiah instantly wished he'd never said a word.

"What makes you think so, eh?" Papa said.

Josiah didn't know what he would have answered if the clumping of boots on the bridge hadn't jerked both their heads toward Nathaniel Putnam and his son, Jonathon.

"Perambulating, Hutchinson?" Nathaniel said.

"Aye," said Papa.

"Why are you doing it on my property?"

And before Joseph Hutchinson could answer, Nathaniel Putnam reached behind him and pulled a gun from his shoulder.

✝ ✦ ✝

Chapter Six

There was a stunned silence as Nathaniel Putnam's musket glinted in the sun. Josiah felt his feet freezing to the bridge beneath him.

"Good heavens, man!" Papa burst out. "Have you gone mad?"

"No, Hutchinson, I think I've finally gone smart! You're standing on my land, and by heaven I want you off. It's time the Putnams stood up for themselves and took back what's rightfully theirs."

At least, that was what Josiah *thought* Nathaniel said. It was difficult to concentrate with the barrel of a gun pointing at your nose. But when Papa spoke, his voice was calm.

"And how do you see this land as being rightfully yours?" Papa said. "Porter has had his mill on it for years, and as you know, half of it now belongs to me. I hear no Putnam in that."

"Of course you don't!" Nathaniel cried as he gave the musket another wave. Josiah followed the barrel with terrified eyes. "You've turned deaf to everything that came before you found your fortune, Hutchinson! But before the beating of the bounds this year, I took myself to Salem Town and looked at the town records. There it was—my father's name on the deed to this very land you're standing on! Now I'll thank you to get off of it, Joseph Hutchinson. And you'd best get you to Israel Porter's to discuss how you're going to remove that sawmill from it!"

Josiah's heart began to pound, and he could feel his eyes bugging from his head. *Could this be true? How?*

But the questions stopped as the gun barrel slowly moved toward Papa's head. Behind Nathaniel Putnam, his son pulled out his own weapon—a shiny, wicked-looking hunting knife whose blade glittered like evil in the spring sunlight. Josiah sucked in air as Jonathon crossed his arms and held the knife threateningly against his own sleeve.

"Get you gone, Hutchinson!" Nathaniel fairly screamed. "And your boy with you!"

Josiah was more than willing to obey that order, but Papa didn't move. When he spoke, his voice was still soft. "I'm not a man foolish enough to argue with a loaded weapon, Nathaniel," he said. "If you feel you must control me in that way, my son and I have no choice but to be gone. But I choose to stay and have this out with you in words. Will you put the gun down?"

Some of the scarlet drained out of Nathaniel's face. Slowly, he lowered his musket from Papa's head, and Josiah felt himself start to shake.

"All right, then," Nathaniel said, his voice teetering, "but we have nothing more to say. This land belongs to the Putnams! I saw it there on paper in plain ink."

"And what was the date on that paper?" Papa said gently.

"Date?" Nathaniel's face puckered. "Why, 'twas sixteen and sixty-one—"

"Thirty years ago."

"Aye! But a deed is good for life—"

"If the land is not sold."

Nathaniel's eyes were riveted on Papa.

"If you had looked further among those town documents," Josiah's father went on, "you would have discovered that in sixteen and eighty-one, this property was sold to Israel Porter."

"Why would my father sell the only—"

Nathaniel stopped and bit his lip.

"The only good land the Putnams ever owned?" Papa finished for him. Still his voice was kind. "For the only reason there could be, Nathaniel—because he was in desperate need of money."

"My father was never desperate for anything!" Nathaniel cried.

"Not until he tried to invest in ironworks and found himself hopelessly entangled. Old Putnam was a farmer, not a businessman. He had to either sell his most valuable land or become a beggar in the streets of Salem Village."

"That's not true!"

"I'm sorry, Nathaniel," Papa said softly, "but it is."

Josiah could hardly bear to look at Nathaniel Putnam. His big, coarse features twisted until Josiah thought the man would cry. Quickly, Josiah looked away, only to catch the eye of Jonathon Putnam, who was still clutching his knife—and looking for all the world as if he wanted to use it on Josiah's throat. For once, Josiah could understand why. There would be almost nothing worse than seeing your own father shamed in front of his worst enemy.

"Come along, then, Josiah," Papa said quietly.

Josiah hurried after his father over the bridge and toward Ipswich Road. Papa kept his eyes straight ahead, but Josiah stole a quick look over his shoulder.

Nathaniel Putnam stood with his back to them, his big head lowered as he appeared to study his boot tops. Josiah felt the first bit of pity he'd ever felt for a Putnam.

But as he gazed, Jonathon Putnam must have felt Josiah's eyes on him, because he quickly turned. With the instinct of an animal, his hand went to his knife.

Josiah jerked his head away and hurried after his father.

When Josiah brought in the wood for the breakfast fire the next morning, Hope was alone in the kitchen.

"You were right," he said to her.

He waited for her dark eyes to flash merrily, for her to toss her black curls and say, "Of course I was!"

But she just looked at him vaguely and said, "Oh?"

"I think some people are more dangerous than we thought."

Hope turned to the fire to fetch the corn bread and said without interest, "Do you now?"

"Aye, anyone who would pull a knife on you—"

The pan of corn bread clattered to the plank floor. Hope whirled around, her eyes wild. "He pulled a knife on you? Jonathon Putnam pulled a knife on you?" Hope was almost screaming. "I told you to be careful, Josiah!"

"How did you know I was talking about Jonathon Putnam?"

Hope stopped cold, and her hands came up to her mouth.

"Hope, how did you know?" Josiah said again.

"What in the name of heaven—?" said a voice behind them.

Hope sprang to life and scrambled to pick up the scattered corn bread as Papa's big shoulders cleared the doorway.

"Josiah," Papa said sternly, "you've been told not to tease your sister when she's about her work. And why are you not about yours?"

"I'm sorry, sir," Josiah said, and he began to unload his firewood onto the small pile on the hearth. All the while, he kept his eyes on Hope. Her face was entirely white, except for the dark, half-moon circles under her eyes. And Josiah knew where those came from. Last night was the third night in a row she had awakened him screaming at the end of some hideous nightmare.

Mama hurried into the kitchen. "What happened?" she said to Hope.

"Ach. I'm just a clumsy ox," Hope said.

"Driven on by an ornery brother," Papa said dryly. "Will there be any breakfast on the table this morning?"

"Aye, Papa," Hope said faintly.

Josiah bent down to help her pick up the last of the corn bread. Did no one else in this house notice that his sister was acting strange? He peeked over at her. Who could miss that look of fear plastered all over her face?

"I'd thought to send Hope to Israel Porter's this morning with some herbs," Mama was saying to Papa. "They're all nearly worn thin there with taking care of him."

"Aye, 'tis a good thought," Papa said.

Beside him, Josiah felt Hope go wooden.

"Must I go, Mama?" she said.

Three pairs of eyes turned to her in shock.

"*Must* you go?" Papa said. "If your mother asks you to, yes, you must go!"

But Mama bent down and gently pulled her up. "What is it, child?" She studied Hope's face. "Are you ill? Have you a fever? I—"

"I'll go, Mama," Josiah said suddenly. He quickly looked at Papa. "I can be back in time to plow."

"Well, *someone* go—and now," Papa said. "We must help the Porters all we can. They've been good friends to us, and we can say that about few in this town. You can get word to Giles while you're there. Tell him we'll need him after dinner."

Josiah's heart sank.

"Good, then, Josiah," Mama said. "Eat your breakfast first."

As he slid into his chair, Josiah stifled a sigh. His eyes caught Hope's across the table.

She was looking straight at him, and she mouthed something.

Be careful, she said silently. *Please be careful.*

Josiah set out after breakfast with a basket of herbs from his mother's garden. As Mama had loaded it up, he'd recognized rue—for old Israel's breathing problems, Mama had explained—and sage, because that always seemed to help. As he ran across Hadlock's Bridge, he wondered if there was anything in the garden to help what was ailing Hope.

But as he rounded the curve in Ipswich Road and saw the Porter house, other thoughts crowded into Josiah's mind. What if Ezekiel or Rachel answered his knock? Would they shove him down the steps—or worse, turn their backs on him? He had spoken barely a word to either of them since last winter, when they'd abandoned the Merry Band. Even after that day in church when Ezekiel had come to his aid, he wasn't sure about him. Ezekiel still hadn't apologized for what he'd done.

It was their mother, Prudence Porter, who met Josiah at the door and smiled down at the basket of herbs.

"Deborah Hutchinson is a saint," she said.

"Yes, ma'am," Josiah mumbled. "Good day, then." He wanted to get away before he ran into Ezekiel.

But Prudence Porter said, "Surely you'll want to come in and bid good day to Israel. It's certain he'll have some message for your father."

"Yes, ma'am," Josiah mumbled again, and he followed her swishing gray skirts into the house and down the hall toward the Porters' best room. *He must be pretty close to death to be bedded down in there*, Josiah thought. A Puritan best room was reserved for Sundays and weddings—and funerals.

Josiah stopped short in the doorway. There in front of him, tightening the ropes on Israel's bed, were Ezekiel and Rachel.

"'Tis young Hutchinson to see you," Prudence sang out to her father-in-law.

Josiah was only vaguely aware that Israel Porter was packed into a chair while his grandchildren restretched the ropes that served as springs on the bed. He could look only at his two former friends, who looked back at him out of the big Porter eyes that seemed to take up half their faces.

"I'll sleep tight now, with those two at work," Israel said. His voice was faint and wheezing. Josiah turned to him and stifled a gasp. In spite of his age, old Israel Porter had always cut a striking figure in Salem Village with his sharp, alert face and his straight, confident shoulders. Now he seemed to be folded into the chair, and the eyes that struggled to focus on Josiah were faded and sunken into his head.

"My mother hopes these herbs will . . . will serve you well, sir," Josiah said.

"Aye, it's sure they will," Prudence said, patting Israel's hand. "He'll be up and barking at us in no time."

"Ach!" Israel cried—and then coughed until he doubled over in the chair. "You're a foolish girl, Prudence," he wheezed. "I'll never be up again and you know it." He waved a frail hand at his grandchildren. "These are the ones who'll be barking now."

Josiah began to edge toward the door, but old Israel feebly waved a finger at him. "I've a message for your father, young man."

"Aye, sir?"

"Tell him—it won't be long now."

Josiah wasn't sure what that meant, but he nodded as he backed out of the room.

"My father had a message for you, too. He'll need Giles after dinner today."

Old Israel nodded and waved him off.

As Josiah hurried down the hall, he heard Prudence Porter say, "You children be sure there are no bedbugs in that mattress."

"Sleep tight, and don't let the bedbugs bite," old Israel gasped out.

When Josiah reached the front yard again, his steps slowed. He'd spent many happy hours here, before Joseph

Putnam had moved their school to his new estate on the other side of the village. On fall afternoons, he, William, and Ezekiel had all gathered here around their teacher, where they had been allowed to ask any question they wished. It was also here that Josiah and Ezekiel had wrestled among the leaves and rolled together in the snow. All of that seemed to be gone forever now.

"He's going to die," said a voice behind him.

Josiah whirled around.

"My grandfather is going to die," Ezekiel said from the porch.

✢ ✤ ✢

Chapter Seven

"Perhaps not," Josiah said. "Perhaps those herbs—"

"My grandfather is always right. If he says he's going to die . . . " Ezekiel couldn't say the rest. He chewed on his lip, and Josiah knew he was fighting to keep back the tears. There was almost nothing worse than crying in front of someone, and in spite of himself, Josiah suddenly wanted to make him feel better.

"Thank you for saving me from Deacon Putnam that day," he blurted out. "I'd have been whipped sure if you hadn't spoken up."

Ezekiel shrugged. "I hate to see the Putnams win—ever."

Josiah stiffened. "Is that the only reason you did it?"

"What other reason would I have?" Ezekiel said, studying his boot top.

"I thought—" Josiah stopped and swallowed hard. "I thought perhaps it was to make up for . . . for what you did to William and me last winter."

"Will you never forget that, Josiah Hutchinson?"

"Aye! When you admit you were wrong!"

"I did nothing wrong!" Ezekiel's face with its sharp Porter cheekbones was as red as any Putnam's. "Even my grandfather said I did nothing wrong!"

"Then your grandfather is mistaken!" Josiah shouted back.

"Take that back! Take that back about my grandfather!"

"Nay!" Josiah could feel his own face going crimson as he yelled at Ezekiel. "Nay, I'll never take it back!"

With that, he turned away. But before he got two steps, he was on his face on the ground with Ezekiel on his back, pounding away at him with his fists.

"Take that back, mongrel!" Ezekiel was screaming through his tears. "Take it back, I say!"

Josiah squirmed beneath him and managed to get onto his back so he could block Ezekiel's flying fists with his own. Ezekiel was wiry and strong, but Josiah had more weight, and with one shove at Ezekiel's shoulders, Josiah had him on his back. They rolled together, kicking and punching and biting.

"Stop this! Stop now!" said a voice from above them.

Before Josiah could look up, he was being yanked from the ground by the back of his shirt.

"What is this madness?" Joseph Putnam cried. "What is this about now?"

Josiah looked from Ezekiel to his teacher and back again, but he couldn't speak yet. Both of them were panting like worn-out dogs.

"Have you taken leave of your senses?" Joseph said.

Josiah shook his head.

"Then what else am I to think when I come upon two of

my prize pupils brawling on the lawn like a pair of mongrel dogs?" He shook his head. "I thought I taught you something about the way educated men behave. I see that I was wrong."

"But what was I to do?" Josiah cried. "He jumped on my back!"

"He insulted my grandfather!"

Joseph's eyebrows shot up. "Aye, I see it all now! Those seem like perfectly good reasons for you to try to kill each other!"

Josiah stared down at the torn knees of his breeches, and he knew Ezekiel was doing the same. Next to his father, there was no one Josiah looked up to more than Joseph Putnam. This was the man who had proven to him that he wasn't a brainless boy, and now he'd acted just like one, right in front of him.

"I know you two have had your differences," Joseph said, "but I always had hope you'd settle them. I never thought to see you going at things this way."

"He wants something from me I cannot give," Ezekiel said stubbornly.

"Ah, and so you jumped him."

"Aye, I did."

To Josiah's surprise, Joseph reached over and took Ezekiel by the back of the shirt, and then did the same to him. He pushed both of them to the front steps and planted them there, side by side. Before either of them could wriggle away, Joseph stood in front of them, arms folded across his chest.

His oak-colored hair shone in the sun as he surveyed them both for a minute. Finally, he said, "I've had differences with a close friend, too. I've been stubborn and refused to give an inch, even though it meant that friend would not be able to see his own granddaughter."

Josiah knew Joseph was talking about Israel. Joseph had married Ezekiel's cousin Constance. When Joseph and Israel had disagreed last winter over what was to be done about the Salem Village church, Israel had vowed that if Joseph didn't do things his way, the child Joseph and Constance were soon going to have wouldn't receive a penny of his money when he died—and neither would Constance.

"I have held fast," Joseph Putnam went on, "because I thought it was right to stand by what I believed no matter what." He leaned in so his face was close to Josiah's and Ezekiel's. "But now I have very little time left to let him know that even though I have not changed my mind about what I believe, I have changed my heart about the way I feel about him."

His words soaked into Josiah's mind like rain into soil. Joseph straightened and looked at them, though not so sternly now. "It's certain there will be harsh words between us these few minutes hence," he said, "but it's also certain old Israel and I will not come to blows, eh?"

Quietly, he put a hand on each of their heads as he stepped over them and went into the house. Silence fell over the boys until Josiah said, "Well, then—"

But Ezekiel stood up and looked down at him. "I'll prove to you that I'm no coward, Josiah Hutchinson!"

Turning on his heel, he darted around the side of the house, leaving Josiah to stare after him.

As Josiah trudged slowly along the Ipswich Road toward home, loneliness wrapped around him like a too-tight jacket.

His head was hanging so low that he didn't see the wagon until he was almost on top of it. *What is a wagon still hitched to its horse doing in the middle of the road anyway?* he thought.

A quick inspection gave him the answer. One of its wheels was mired halfway to the axle in the spring mud. Josiah felt sorry for the owner. It wasn't easy to get a wagon out of a fix like this if you didn't know how.

He looked around, but the owner was nowhere in sight. Deciding that it must be an old woman who wasn't strong enough to tackle the job and had gone for help, Josiah searched for and found a small, sturdy oak log. Carefully, he placed it at the edge of the stuck wheel and wiggled it until it dug into the mud and under the wheel. Holding the end that stuck out, he pressed down. The wheel moved up easily, but as soon as he let go, it sank again.

Josiah rocked back on his heels. This would be much easier if he had someone to drive the horse forward while he pushed down on his lever.

He looked up at the horse, a bony mare who was waiting patiently with her head nearly dragging on the ground.

"Hey now," Josiah called softly to her. "Giddyap now, would you? Giddyap, girl."

Without interest, the horse looked at him over her shoulder.

"Giddyap now, whatever your name is."

"Her name is Gussie," said a tiny voice.

Josiah turned to see a pale face peering at him from over the side of the wagon. It was Betty Parris. With a jerk, Josiah pulled his hands away from the wheel.

"Is this Reverend Parris's wagon?" he said.

"Aye, and we're stuck."

Josiah looked around warily. "Where is your father?"

"He went for help," she said in her tiny, brittle voice.

Josiah looked up at her in surprise. "Why didn't he just make a lever and have you drive the horse? It isn't that stuck."

"Look how muddy that has gotten you," she said. "He says that would never do for a minister."

Josiah looked down at the icky ooze that slimed the front of his breeches. It was just mud. A few minutes with some water and sand, and it would come right out. To leave a wagon in the middle of the road to avoid a little mud seemed silly to Josiah.

"Can you get it out?" Betty said.

Her voice was small and fragile, but Josiah liked to hear it. It was almost like a miniature bell tinkling from far away.

"I can," he said, "but I don't know if I should. Perhaps your father wouldn't like it."

She smiled as if she had a secret. "He was very angry when this happened. He would be happy for anyone to fix it."

"Well, not anyone," Josiah said. He looked up at her again. She was resting her delicate chin on her arms, which she'd folded neatly on the edge of the wagon. Her pale eyes were shimmering. She didn't look all that sickly to Josiah.

"I'll fix it," he said, "but you mustn't tell your father who did it."

"I don't know who did it," she said. "I don't know your name, except you're a Hutchinson."

"Don't even tell him that much," Josiah said quickly. "Just tell him—tell him it was the Good Samaritan."

She nodded happily.

"Now, you can help me. I mean, if you know how to drive the horse."

Her eyes almost sparkled. "I do, though no one knows it. I just watch carefully."

"All right, then," Josiah said. "Take hold of the reins, and when I tell you, you coax her forward. Not too fast."

"Not too fast," Betty murmured. She stepped daintily to the driver's seat and picked up the reins in her fairylike hands.

Josiah pressed down on the oak log and shouted, "Go!"

"Giddyap, Gussie," Betty said softly.

Josiah groaned to himself. No horse would move an inch on a command like that. But Gussie clopped slowly forward, and Josiah jounced down on the lever. The wheel rose easily out of the mud and up onto the drier land.

Betty gently pulled the horse to a halt and turned around to look at him.

"You are the Good Samaritan!" she said.

Josiah shrugged and hurled the log harder than he had to into the trees.

"Remember now," he called to her as he slipped into the woods, "it was the Good Samaritan."

"Aye!" she called back. And he knew she watched him until he disappeared.

Josiah felt himself strutting through his chores the rest of the morning. But the puff went out of his chest when he headed for the barn after dinner to hitch the oxen to the plow and found Giles Porter already at it. After fighting with Ezekiel and rescuing Betty Parris, he'd forgotten what the afternoon was going to bring.

"Ah, it's the injured one!" Giles said.

It always sounded to Josiah as if Giles were about to burst into song before some admiring congregation. Josiah just grunted.

"We'll make short work of this planting," Giles was saying. "I'll plow the rows, and you can walk behind and drop the seeds in, eh?"

Every nerve in Josiah's body seemed to stand on end. He crossed his arms over his chest to keep them from popping through his skin.

Giles brought up one corner of his mouth. "You've done that with your papa, haven't you, boy?"

"Aye," Josiah said, "but I thought I was to—"

"To what?"

Giles stood looking down at him with his hands on his narrow hips. His big chest rose and fell evenly as he waited for Josiah to answer.

"I thought I was to do the plowing—some of it anyway."

Giles looked at him for a minute as the other corner of his mouth went up. The sharp Porter cheekbones nearly poked through his face as the grin grew wider. Suddenly, he jerked his head back and began to laugh.

Why is that funny? Josiah's thoughts cried out. But he said nothing as Giles chuckled to a stop and grinned down at him with his gray eyes watering.

"Get your bucket, boy," he said, still chortling. "I don't want to have to pick you up out of the mud again, eh?"

With that, he slapped the oxen's flanks and led them toward the field. Josiah picked up the seed bucket, but not before he soundly kicked a bale of hay.

When Josiah got back to the house that evening, Hope was sitting on the back step, poking a needle in and out of a piece of cloth like a chicken pecking angrily at a bug. Josiah recognized the feeling. He'd been putting seed into the ground the same way all afternoon.

"It's just cloth," Josiah said as he stopped nearby to gather the evening's wood. "It won't bite back."

"These are your breeches I'm mending, Josiah, so I'd be careful what I said, were I you."

"I did wash them myself," he snapped.

"Aren't you just a saint, then," Hope said. Josiah shrugged, and she continued. "I don't see how you can tear out both your knees just going to Israel Porter's with a basket of herbs."

"I got into a fight with Ezekiel Porter."

Her head jerked up. "Was it about what happened last winter?"

"Aye."

Hope stopped sewing and narrowed her eyes at him. "Who won?"

"No one. Joseph Putnam stopped us before that was decided."

"Oh." Hope looked disappointed. "I wish you had. Ezekiel should be made to pay for what he did. He's as bad as the Putnams for leaving you and William at their mercy. To possibly be—" She stopped and returned to her sewing with a vengeance. "So where were you fighting—in the hogs' pen?"

"No." Josiah picked up the last of the wood and turned to her. "I got the mud from helping Betty Parris get her father's wagon out of a rut. You know how the Ipswich Road muddies in spring. . . . " Josiah trailed off. Even as he watched, the color washed out of Hope's face and the fear sprang back into her eyes.

"Parris!" she said.

"Aye, but the reverend was nowhere around. He won't even know 'twas me. I made Betty promise not to tell."

"You can't trust her! You can't trust any of them! Not the Parrises and not the Putnams! I told you that, Josiah!" The breeches had slipped to the ground, and Hope clutched her hands.

"All right, then, I won't trust them," Josiah said. He would have said anything to keep her from flying off the steps.

She stared at him hard for a minute and then leaned over to pick up her sewing. "Just you remember," she said, "they're more dangerous than we ever dreamed."

✝ ⬥ ✝

Chapter Eight

As the Hutchinsons gathered around the breakfast table the next morning, Papa looked curiously around the room. "What is that knocking?" he said.

Josiah heard it, too—a tiny tapping from the direction of the front door.

"See about it, Hope," Papa said.

As Hope went to the door, Josiah dug back into his trencher of mush. He almost wished Hope wouldn't eat all of hers. He was starving this morning.

"What in heaven's name?" Papa said.

Josiah looked up. Hope was standing in the kitchen doorway. In her arms was a frightened Dorcas Carrier.

Mama hurried over to her, immediately cooing and purring. Josiah made a dash for the window. If Dorcas was here, Deliverance couldn't be far away.

Behind him, Dorcas began to whimper.

"Hush now, little one," Mama said softly. "Where is your mama?"

That's what I would like to know, Josiah thought as he craned his neck at the window. Deliverance was nowhere in sight.

"Josiah," Hope said. "I think she wants you."

Josiah turned around. Dorcas was straining from Mama's arms with her two little dirty paws stretched out toward him. She whimpered and smiled at the same time, and no one in the room could have denied that she wanted him to take her.

Reluctantly, Josiah crossed the room, and the baby scrambled into his arms and hugged his neck.

"'Tis as if she knew you," Papa said.

"She does," Josiah said miserably. "She's Deliverance Carrier's girl."

"Deliverance Carrier?" Papa said.

"Aye." Josiah looked at Hope. "She's the one we allowed to stay in the Widow Hooker's cabin."

"Ah," Papa said, crossing to the window, "then where is the woman?"

"She still lives in the cabin," Josiah said. "I—I took some food to her just the other day. That's how she . . . that's how Dorcas knows me."

"She certainly took a liking to you," Mama said. "You'll be a fine father someday, Josiah."

Josiah looked wildly at his mother and peeled Dorcas away from him. "Please take her!" he said.

Hope smothered a laugh and reached for Dorcas. "Come, little one. I think you could use some breakfast. She can have the rest of mine, Mama."

Josiah looked forlornly at his sister's trencher as Hope sat down next to it and Dorcas began to stuff its contents into her mouth with both hands.

"So where is this Carrier woman?" Papa said to Josiah. "What do you know of her?"

Josiah shrugged. "She's near to starving to death up there, but when you try to help her, she's not very grateful."

"And terrified to come to anyone's house for help, I'll warrant you," Goodman Hutchinson said. "Especially with the likes of the Putnams slamming doors in beggars' faces, calling them children of the devil."

Mama looked over at Dorcas. "It's sure that's no devil's child," she said.

Papa watched the little girl thoughtfully for a minute. "I can think only one thing, Deborah," he said. "Her mother's left her on our doorstep to care for her."

"Do you think she'll be back?" Mama said.

Papa looked at Josiah. "What say you?"

"Aye, it's sure she will," Josiah said. Deliverance Carrier did her share of screeching at the child, but she had been frantic that day when she'd thought her daughter had been carried off.

"Then we must find the woman and see that both of them are fed," Papa said. "No child should be separated from its mother, eh?"

"Aye," Mama said. She bustled across the kitchen and began to fold food into a napkin. "Hope," she said over her shoulder, "go to the cabin and find this Goody Carrier. Take the child."

"And bring them both back if they're willing," Papa said. "Perhaps there's work she can do around here."

"Aye," Mama said. Standing with her back to Hope, wrapping bundles of food, she couldn't see the fear that froze her daughter's face. "You must go," she said. "I can see to the morning's work without you for once."

Josiah watched his sister. A month earlier, she would have leapt at a chance to be out on a spring day, even if it meant hauling a two-year-old on her back. But Hope's face grew pasty, and her eyes darted with fear.

Josiah looked quickly at his father. "Perhaps I should go, too, Papa," he said. "'Tis a long way—" But he stopped, because the minute he began to speak, Dorcas looked adoringly at him, porridge dripping from her chin, and held out her thin little arms.

Mama laughed softly. "Perhaps it *would* be a good idea for Josiah to go along, Joseph. Hope might have her hands full otherwise."

Josiah's father's eyes took on a rare twinkle. "Good, then. You go as well—Little Papa."

Josiah could feel his cheeks burning. If he hadn't wanted to protect his sister so much, he would have bolted from the room like a shot from a musket. Hope had just better be grateful.

As they headed up Thorndike Hill, each carrying a bundle of food and Dorcas trotting behind them, Hope took hold of Josiah's arm and didn't let go until they had reached Topsfield. Even when Dorcas whimpered and sat down among the buttercups and daisies on the side of Davenport Hill to rest, Hope curled her fingers around Josiah's sleeve and kept her eyes flitting all around her.

"What are you so afraid of?" Josiah said. "It's broad daylight."

"That makes no difference, Josiah," she said. "You just don't know."

"No," Josiah said, "and I won't unless you tell me."

"Let's go," she said firmly. "We must get this baby to her mother." She reached down to pick up Dorcas, but the little girl scrambled unsteadily to her feet and threw her arms around Josiah's legs.

"She wants you to carry her," Hope said. "Now do it and let's be gone."

With one more frightened glance over her shoulder, Hope grabbed Josiah's arm and pulled him on. He shifted Dorcas onto one hip and followed.

Josiah almost kissed the ground when they finally reached the last stand of trees before the widow's cabin. It was a long walk under any conditions, and with Dorcas asleep against his chest, it was like making the trek with a 20-pound bag of flour.

But when they reached the edge of the trees and looked out across the clearing, his heart plummeted to his toes. Beside him, Hope gasped, and Dorcas startled awake in his arms.

There before them were the remains of the Widow Hooker's cabin. Every plank, every board, every shingle was scattered about the clearing, the pieces jagged and broken from the blade of an ax. Josiah felt his eyes bulging from their sockets as he slowly set Dorcas on the ground. The cabin . . . the widow's cabin. He felt as if his heart had been chopped up with it.

"First the Blessing Place, now this!" Josiah said.

"I don't care about silly meeting places!" Hope cried. "Don't you see? This is a warning!"

"From who?"

"Who *else?*" Hope's voice teetered dangerously on the edge of panic. "It was the Putnams, Josiah! It's a warning from the Putnams!" Her voice caught and Dorcas began to whimper. "I told you, they're more dangerous than we ever thought. I told you, Josiah! I told you!"

Josiah grabbed Hope by the arm and pulled her back toward the trees. "Let's go home, then," he said. "Come on, let's go."

"We have to run, Josiah!" she said. "Please!"

Before he could answer, she was flying out in front of him with her hand still gripping his wrist. He grabbed Dorcas up and stumbled after her.

"I see nothing else to do but to keep her here until Deliverance Carrier returns for her," Papa said that evening.

Josiah glanced over at little Dorcas, who was asleep in Mama's lap. *At least she's drooling on someone else for a change*, Josiah thought. His father's words weren't the happiest he could hear right now. Ever since they had returned home, Dorcas had followed him all over the farm. He didn't even attempt to get Giles to let him drive the plow—not with her clinging to his breeches.

"We've a friend with us today, eh?" Giles had sung out. Josiah hadn't missed the smirk that played at the edges of Giles's practiced smile.

As if that hadn't been enough, Dorcas had insisted on sitting next to Josiah at the table, and she had even napped in a pile of hay in the barn while he'd fed the livestock.

"Josiah," his father said now, "I must go at sunrise to Salem Town to do some business. Before you start your morning's work, go you to the sawmill and tell Benjamin Porter I won't be there."

At least that meant he could get away from Giles Porter for a while. The night's rain stopped in the wee hours of the morning, and the daisies and buttercups that bordered the roads were just lifting their heads as Josiah hurried toward the sawmill right after breakfast. The delicious spring air filled his chest, and he felt free for a change . . . until he heard the familiar whimpering behind him.

"Oh, no," he muttered before he even turned around. When he did look, there was Dorcas, tripping through the wildflowers with her arms held out toward him.

"No, Dorcas!" Josiah called to her. "You can't come with me. Go back!"

"Josiah!" It was Hope's voice coming from the kitchen door. "Is Dorcas with you?"

"Aye," Josiah called back.

"Good. Mama says to see that you watch over her." And then the door slammed, and Dorcas gazed up at him out of her pale, worshiping eyes. A small, almost invisible hand crept into his.

"Come on, then," Josiah mumbled. "I just pray no one sees us."

That prayer was answered on the way to the sawmill. Even Benjamin Porter was so busy with his work that he seemed not to notice the child as Josiah delivered his father's message.

But as he was hurrying back along the Frost Fish River with Dorcas grasping his hand and tripping behind him, he heard a rustling in the brush. Before the thought of a bear could even spring into his mind, Richard Putnam stepped into their path. Dorcas wrapped herself around Josiah's leg.

"Well, well, what have we here?" Richard said, his lip curling back almost to his nose.

Dorcas whined and held on tight. *She's a smart little thing,* Josiah thought. *She knows a rat when she meets one.*

"Doing the women's work now, eh, Hutchinson?" Richard said. "It's about time your family recognized your real abilities."

Richard was the only Putnam with a quick wit and a sharp tongue to match. Unfortunately, lively words weren't one of Josiah's gifts. Strong legs and a fast getaway—now those were his strong suits. *That is, when I don't have somebody's child hanging from my thigh,* he thought. Dorcas was climbing up his shin and crying in earnest.

"Well, pick her up, *Mama,*" Richard said. He took a step forward. "Or shall I take her for you while you run for help? After all, you're not much good without your little band of robbers, are you?"

Josiah's eyes darted behind Richard and across the river. Richard was bigger—and certainly meaner—than he was. Running really was the only thing to do. But the question was where, and how, with Dorcas barely able to keep up at a walk?

And then his eyes caught on something moving amid the trees just to their right. There it was again, where the leaves didn't yet cover the branches. There was something white lurking near the trunk of an oak, and it made a scratching noise.

Richard heard it, too, for his head jerked toward the sound.

"Bear!" Josiah cried out. "It's a bear! Run!"

Before Josiah could even think about taking off, Richard had gone past him and was crashing through the trees behind him. Josiah didn't wait to see how he fared. He scooped Dorcas onto his back and drove straight ahead, past the spot where the "bear" had been clawing at the tree bark.

It wasn't a bear at all, he knew. There were no white bears in *these* woods, as far as he knew. Someone had played a fine trick on Richard Putnam. Hurrying toward home with Dorcas bouncing on his back, Josiah wondered who it had been.

About halfway to the Hutchinson farm, Josiah slowed to a trot. He'd been so anxious to get away, he hadn't thought about how Dorcas was doing, jouncing up and down against his shoulders like a sack of sugar. As he shifted her weight, he heard a sound he hadn't heard coming from her before. It was like the bubbling of water in one of their brooks. Dorcas Carrier was laughing.

"What's so funny?" he said as he picked up his pace again.

She jostled against his shoulder blades and gurgled like springwater.

"You think that's hilarious, do you?" he said. "Come on, then, let's really hear you!"

He broke into a run that sent her bouncing up and down. All the way home she laughed, until by the time they reached the kitchen she was hiccuping and gasping for air.

"Really, Josiah," Hope said as she took Dorcas from him. "She isn't a bag of feed."

Josiah shrugged. He was pretty sure Dorcas would be anything he wanted her to be. And that wasn't such a bad feeling.

✠ ⬧ ✠

Chapter Nine

Almost a week passed and there was still no sign of Deliverance Carrier. The Hutchinsons' little guest began to fall into a routine—most of it made up of following Josiah around the farm. He spent almost as much time making grass whistles for her and picking her up off the ground as he did working at his chores.

He gave up on asking Giles to let him plow, and for the last days of planting, he stomped along behind, dumping seeds into the furrows while Dorcas chirped at his heels. By the end of the week, the planting was done and at sunset that day, Papa met them in the barn and put out his hand to Giles.

"Your help has been a blessing to us," Joseph Hutchinson said.

"As has yours to us," young Giles said. "My uncle Benjamin doesn't have your business sense. Without you there to run the sawmill in Grandfather's absence, who knows what might happen, eh?"

They walked out into the dusk—*as if I weren't even here*, Josiah thought.

Resentment burned his cheeks as he untied the ropes from the oxen and nearly tripped over Dorcas in the process. She grabbed at his leg and held on.

"Does she think you're her mother?" said a voice from the doorway.

Josiah looked up to see William grinning at him. Josiah ground his teeth together and said, "Shut it, William."

"I heard she follows you everywhere."

"Just shut it."

William backed up, but his eyes were still twinkling. "All right, Mama!"

Why can't we leave her on somebody else's doorstep, Josiah thought as he chased William from the barn.

With the planting done, Josiah was at loose ends by mid-morning the next day.

Papa was off to the sawmill as usual, and Mama and Hope were busy sanding clean the planks of the kitchen floor, when Josiah crept in and said, "May I have leave to search for Deliverance Carrier? My work's done 'til supper."

"Aye," Mama said, "and take the child with you. Her sweet face may soften some of these stiff-necked people."

Josiah watched Dorcas, who was already headed for the door. He hated dragging her along. He could go so much faster without her clinging to his leg saying, "'Siah."

But perhaps Mama was right. She might tug at someone's heart, and maybe he could get her back to her mother and out of his hair.

By the time the sun was straight over his head, Josiah had knocked on the door of every house in their part of the village that didn't belong to a Putnam. No one he talked to had seen little Dorcas's mother.

"What a precious child," many of the goodwives said.

"And what a precious little mama," some of their sons whispered.

Some things spread faster than smallpox, Josiah thought to himself. Heading back to the Hutchinson farm, Josiah suddenly stopped with a jolt that set Dorcas to giggling on his back. He bounced absently to keep her laughing and stared straight ahead at the parsonage.

The Parris house was the only non-Putnam home he hadn't visited. The Reverend Parris was a puppet of the Putnams, that was sure. But he was still a minister. Surely, if he had seen Deliverance Carrier, he would have given her food and seen that she had shelter. He *had* preached about the Good Samaritan, after all.

Josiah took a deep breath and headed for the minister's front door. His knock echoed emptily, but the door finally opened. To his surprise, Betty Parris stood before him.

Her frail face broke into a smile. "Good day!" she said in her tiny-bell voice. "'Tis my rescuer!"

Josiah barely got his finger to his lips to beg her silence when Abigail Williams appeared in the doorway, her green eyes narrowed down at him.

"Rescuer from what?" she demanded.

"Who is this?" Betty said instead, her pale-blue eyes shimmering on Josiah's little companion.

"'Tis Dorcas Carrier," Josiah said quickly as Betty stepped

out into the sunlight and bent down in front of the little girl.

"Is she a cousin of yours?" Betty said.

"No!" Abigail answered for him. "She's that wretched beggar woman's child. Don't touch her, Betty! She's likely to have some disease."

"She has nothing of the kind!" Josiah said sharply.

Abigail's eyebrows shot up. "Ah! The brainless boy speaks! 'Tis a rare occasion!" She thumped Josiah sharply on the shoulder. "'Tis true you would know if the child has a disease. It's said you *are* her mama."

Just then a dark figure bustled up behind Abigail, scolding in gibberish and shaking her finger. Josiah recognized Tituba, the Parris family's slave woman from the West Indian island of Barbados. She was as black as the shadows in the front hall, but her eyes flashed angrily at Abigail—until she saw Dorcas.

"Ah ba-bee!" she exclaimed. She stooped to look into the child's face. Josiah expected Dorcas to climb up his leg in fear, but she just blinked at Tituba and studied her black face carefully.

"Here!" Tituba said suddenly. "Dis for you!"

She dug into her apron and pulled out a round, brown object that she tucked into Dorcas's mouth. Josiah's own mouth watered. If he didn't miss his guess, that was a piece of maple sugar candy, a rare treat for Puritan children. Dorcas sucked on it happily until drool dripped from the corner of her mouth.

"Why have you brought her here, brainless boy?" Abigail said.

"I'm looking for her mother, Deliverance Carrier," Josiah said. "Have you seen her about?"

Abigail's lip curled. "It's sure she wouldn't come to this

door. We've naught to do with the likes of her here. This is the parsonage!"

"I—I thought perhaps Reverend Parris would want to—"

"What would the minister want with a child of the devil?"

"This is no devil," Betty said softly.

They all looked down at Betty, who sat on the front stoop with Dorcas in her lap, a trail of gooey maple sugar running from her tiny lips.

"This is an angel," Betty whispered.

Abigail whispered back, "Then let him take his 'angel' and be gone." She turned and disappeared inside the house.

"I'd best be taking her home now," Josiah said to Betty.

Betty's pale eyes drooped, and slowly she held Dorcas up for Josiah to take her.

"Good-bye, angel," she whispered.

Josiah tossed Dorcas over his shoulders, and then stood shifting from one foot to the other. Betty's eyes were so sad.

"I'll bring her back one day," he said suddenly. "I mean, if you want me to."

Betty's eyes lit up like two tiny candle flames. "Aye, I do!"

"Come along *now*, Betty!" Abigail yelled from within. The candle flames went out and Betty sighed.

"She thinks she's the mistress of me," she whispered.

"She thinks she's the mistress of everyone," Josiah said.

The candles flickered again and she smiled.

As Josiah trudged home with Dorcas slung across his back, his mind stumbled over everything that had happened in the past few hours. It seemed there was no trace of Deliverance Carrier in all of Salem Village. And there was no trace of good in Abigail Williams, Josiah was sure of that, too.

But Betty was a Parris, and he decided there wasn't a trace of bad in her. And Tituba, she was no Christian at all to hear the Putnams tell it. Yet she was the only one all day who had offered to give Dorcas so much as a mouthful. What about Reverend Parris himself? Was it true that he preached the gospel of the Good Samaritan on Sunday and turned away beggars from his own door the rest of the week?

"Some?" said a tiny voice in his ear.

Josiah stopped and peeked over his shoulder. "'Siah, some?" Dorcas said again. She stuck out a sticky fist and opened it near Josiah's nose to reveal a lumpy, oozy glob of used maple sugar candy. "You, some!" she sang out happily.

"No, thank you," Josiah said, wrinkling his nose.

She watched him carefully. "Some!" she said insistently.

"No, really, you eat it," he replied meekly.

"Some!"

Josiah opened his mouth, and Dorcas shoved the glob in. He had to admit—a piece of candy had never tasted better. He was trotting across the front yard to the Hutchinson house with Dorcas squealing in his ear, when he saw Mama appear in the doorway. Something about the way her shoulders slumped slowed Josiah to a walk.

"Josiah!" she called out to him in a thin voice. "Come quickly, son. You must take a message to your father."

Slowly, Josiah pulled Dorcas from his shoulders. It was sure he wouldn't be taking her along on this mission, for it was almost certain the news he was delivering was bad.

✦ ✦ ✦

hen Josiah reached the front stoop, he could see
that his mother's eyes were ringed in red.

"Run quickly to the sawmill, Josiah," she said in a
quavery voice. "You must tell your papa that Isaiah Porter has
died. Here—" She held out her arms and took Dorcas. "I'll
keep her here with me."

Josiah stood as if he were rooted to the ground. He would
rather march straight into Richard Putnam's house with
Dorcas clinging to his pant leg crying "Mama" than carry this
news to his father.

"Please, Josiah, go quickly now," Mama said again.

There was nothing else to do but turn and run with lead in
his legs across the yard and down the road toward the sawmill.
But as soon as he turned the corner and headed past the
Hadlock house, his steps grew slower. He kicked at a bunch of
bloodroot growing along the path and sighed heavily.

The Porters never seemed to go through the troubles and
struggles that Josiah's family did. Everything seemed to go

smoothly for them. But they hadn't escaped death, had they? How was Ezekiel feeling now? Josiah couldn't help it—he felt bad for him.

As he neared the sawmill, Josiah's steps grew even slower. What mattered now was that his father had loved the old man, and now Josiah had to be the one to tell him his friend was dead.

Joseph Hutchinson was standing at the saw wheel with his back curved over his work when Josiah reached the sawmill.

"Papa!" he shouted over the ear-splitting sound. "Papa, I've a message for you!"

Two large chunks of a tree clattered to the floor and splinters flew into the air as Papa stopped the blade and looked at him from under his shaggy brows. There was a question etched on his father's face.

"Why are you not at your work, Josiah?" he said. "Is there some trouble?"

"Aye, sir."

"Speak up. What is it?"

Josiah drew his next breath slowly. The words he was about to utter were going to change many things for his father.

Papa's eyes searched him. "What news have you for me, Josiah?"

"'Tis Israel Porter, sir," Josiah said. "He . . ."

But there was no need to go on. Papa closed his eyes and nodded, and the words were left hanging unspoken in the air.

Slowly, Papa turned his back to Josiah and pressed his hands against the saw. "Go along home now," he said. "Tell your mother I'll be home come suppertime. I've much work still to do."

"Aye, sir," Josiah said, and he turned to go. But he had gone only a few steps when he heard something that made his head jerk back toward his father. Papa's face was hanging low over the saw, and from somewhere deep inside him came a sound Josiah had heard only once before. Hard, raspy gasps ripped from within, each ending with a whine of sheer pain. Joseph Hutchinson was crying, the way he had a year ago when it was sure that Hope would die. Only then, he had gone straight to Israel Porter for help. *Now he must feel he has no one to go to anymore*, Josiah thought.

Papa's big shoulders shook, and Josiah couldn't stand to watch. Backing silently away, he left the sawmill and slipped off along the river toward home. But he couldn't shake the picture of Papa from his mind. He was so alone now, and that was a feeling Josiah himself was beginning to know well. Even God seemed far away. Being a man must mean being alone.

Josiah rounded the corner and started up the road to the Hutchinson farm. Even from there he could hear the chirping, and he could see the wispy blonde head bobbing toward him.

"'Siah!" Dorcas's little voice cried.

Josiah looked over both shoulders. There was no one around. He stooped down and held out his arms. As long as no one was watching, he might as well give her a horseback ride.

Israel Porter's funeral was held three days later, on a gray, drizzly afternoon. Josiah was allowed to sit with his mother and sister in the Meeting House instead of up in the gallery. He suspected it was to help keep Dorcas from squirming under the bench or chirping during one of Reverend Parris's prayers. It was obvious Deliverance Carrier had never taken her to church.

"She's next door to a perfect little heathen, isn't she?" Hope whispered to him.

The minister droned on for what seemed like hours to Josiah—all about how sinful people are and how they should all pray that God was merciful and had taken Israel Porter into His kingdom. Finally, the reverend said, "I bid you bow your heads now and go to God with this burden."

But Josiah had a different burden. He shifted Dorcas from one knee to the other, and her head lolled sleepily against his wool jacket. *Lord, please help me find a way to be a man*, he prayed, *so I can stop making trouble for everyone. Maybe you could start by helping me find Deliverance Carrier.*

After the service, the Hutchinsons slogged through the thin rain to the Porters' to pay their respects to the family. Josiah was happy to tumble Dorcas into Prudence Porter's big bed. She seemed twice as heavy when she was sleeping, and besides, she had drooled all down the sleeve of his jacket.

As he left the bedroom and started down the stairs, he noticed that one of his breeches ties had come undone at the knee again. Sighing, he sat down on a step to retie it. He was glad he didn't have to wear these dress-up clothes too often.

As he fumbled with the coarse wool strips, he heard a muffled sound in one of the rooms behind him.

Something pulled Josiah to the sound as if he were being drawn in by a string. He followed it until he was standing outside the door to Ezekiel's room.

Josiah pressed his ear to the closed door and listened.

There was no mistaking it. Someone was crying—hard.

Josiah silently pushed the door open a crack. Ezekiel was lying on his bed, face down, with his fists pounding on his pillows. His head writhed back and forth as he sobbed from somewhere deep inside himself.

Josiah clutched the door. He'd felt like that before, like there was no bottom to the sadness. He could almost feel the same pain that seemed to be coursing through Ezekiel racing through his own chest and grabbing at his throat. He held on hard to the door to keep from running across the room to Ezekiel's bed and snatching him up by the arm and saying, "Come on! Let's go down to the river and throw rocks as hard as we can!"

He put his hand up to stop the tears that stung his eyes. As he did, the door moved and creaked. Ezekiel sat up with a jolt, and red, puffy eyes found Josiah standing in the doorway.

For a moment, Ezekiel only looked sad, and for that same moment, Josiah almost cried out, "Come on! Let's get away from here!"

But the moment was snapped away.

"What do you want?" Ezekiel said.

Josiah didn't know, so he said nothing.

"Get you gone then!" Ezekiel cried. And he threw himself down on the bed again.

Josiah went back to the landing and sank onto one of the top steps. He jammed his head into his hands and sat there until the light that passed through the tiny square window above him had almost winked out. It was then that a voice spoke to him from the landing.

"I see you've found a thinking spot, Captain." Josiah

brought his face up. He didn't have to make out the smile in the gathering gloom to know it was Joseph Putnam.

"Aye, sir," Josiah said.

"I need to do a bit of thinking myself. May I join you?"

Josiah squirmed aside uneasily. "If you want to, sir," he said.

Joseph Putnam's eyebrows arched as he sat beside Josiah on the step. "Why wouldn't I want to join you, Captain? It's been some time since we've talked."

Josiah couldn't look at him. "I didn't think . . . I mean, the last time . . .".

"Ah." Joseph folded his arms across his knees and smiled. "I caught you and young Porter tumbling on old Israel's lawn, preparing to do one another in, eh?"

Josiah nodded miserably.

"I see you've not been able to work out your differences with your friend."

"No, and I probably never will."

"No? Not even though he needs your friendship now more than ever?"

Josiah shifted uncomfortably on the step. "I don't think he wants my friendship."

"And what makes you think that?"

"Because I've told him," Josiah said, staring at the palms of his hands, "that all he has to do is admit that what he did to me and to William was wrong—and I'll forgive him. Is that asking so much?"

"Let me see if I have this right," Joseph said. He cocked his handsome head of oak-colored hair to the side and studied the stairwell carefully. "Ezekiel has committed some dreadful betrayal of your friendship, for which you are willing to forgive him, big-hearted fellow that you are, if he will only crawl a little. Own up to his foul deed and all that."

Josiah stared at his teacher. Was Joseph Putnam, his beloved friend, making fun of him?

But Joseph's face was serious as he looked back at Josiah. "Is that what I hear you saying?" he said.

Josiah nodded, and Joseph Putnam squeezed his arm. "On first hearing, that appears to be very sound reasoning. I used to believe in that way of thinking myself—that there are conditions on forgiveness. I told myself, 'I will forgive him if he does this or that.'" Joseph smiled wryly. "I was wrong about that, though, and unfortunately I learned that too late. I tried to work out my differences with old Israel Porter, but he was far too sick to really understand what I was saying."

"Your wife and your baby won't be in his will then?" Josiah said.

Joseph shook his head. "Worse than that, Captain. Much worse than that. I let a good friend go to his grave without knowing that I forgave him."

There was a long silence. Both Josiah and Joseph studied their hands until the stairwell was almost completely wrapped in darkness and a chill had settled over them both.

"Don't make the same mistake I did, Captain," Joseph said finally. "We must live and act by the teachings we claim to believe, and I don't think that is happening in this village."

He spoke as if a huge lump had formed in his throat, and Josiah looked at him in time to see one tear trickling from the corner of Joseph's eye and shimmering sadly in the faint light.

"Come then, Captain," he said huskily. "It's sure they'll be looking for us both down below."

Josiah dismally followed him down to the Porters' best room. The grown-ups were sitting about, talking in hushed voices. As Josiah lingered in the doorway, he spied Giles by the window, calmly drinking a mug of cider and smoothly gazing around the room. His glance snagged on Josiah, and almost automatically the Porter smile sprang to his lips. He lifted his mug to Josiah and nodded before his eyes glided on around the room.

For someone who loved his grandfather so much, Josiah thought, *he's surely in a happy mood*. Josiah shuddered and headed for the kitchen. He had to squeeze his way through the sea of legs in the hallway to slip into the kitchen where the table was groaning with pies and stews left untouched by the listless mourners. Josiah's mouth watered as he eyed a plate of blueberry tarts, and he was about to slide one inside his woolen jacket when he heard a familiar high-pitched whine in the corner near the fireplace.

"'Tis a fact!" Reverend Parris was crying out. "I tell you, Ingersoll, it was in the agreement I made with these people before I came here. The deed to the parsonage is to come to me."

Thin, shriveled Nathaniel Ingersoll shook his balding head. "I know that, but there are people here who will fight you on that. Every parsonage in all of Massachusetts Colony belongs to the church, not the minister."

"They made an exception in my case! I have it in writing, signed by Thomas Putnam and by—"

"By Joseph Hutchinson?" Nathaniel Ingersoll said.

At the sound of his father's name, Josiah ducked under the table and held his breath. If they were going to talk about Papa, it was sure they didn't want *him* to hear.

"Joseph Hutchinson!" Reverend Parris sputtered. "That Judas Iscariot? Of course not! He never wanted me to come here in the first place."

"But that land on which the parsonage sits once belonged to the Hutchinsons," said Nathaniel Ingersoll. "His father gave it and the property for the Meeting House to the church years ago."

"Then it's no longer his!"

"But he gave it to be owned by the church, not by you."

"I *am* the church!"

Reverend Parris's words exploded over the kitchen and seemed to shake the very table Josiah was hiding under.

"Thomas Putnam thinks the only reason Joseph Hutchinson has come back to the village congregation is to take back his property and leave you and the church in shame. I only warn you that there may be some discord."

"I am accustomed to discord. What I am not accustomed to is the obvious lack of regard for my station here. Why, look you at this—this table shamelessly piled with food. Yet what about the food supplies I was promised when I came here? Is not every resident of this village obliged to provide me with enough to live on so that I may go about the business of saving their souls. I—what is this now?"

With the sudden shift in his voice, Josiah froze and squeezed his eyes shut. In seconds, he felt himself being dragged out from under the table by a pair of very angry hands.

"'Tis you—*again!*" Reverend Parris screeched. "Why must

I come upon you every time I turn 'round?"

He pinched the tip of Josiah's ear and pulled him to his feet. Josiah held his breath to keep from squealing.

"What are you about here, young Hutchinson?" Nathaniel Ingersoll said. "Spying on the minister?"

"Did your father send you?" Reverend Parris said. Josiah tried to shake his head, but Parris kept a tight squeeze on his ear. "Then what are you doing here, boy? What is your business here under this table?"

An awkward pause ensued, until a voice shattered the silence. "Caught again, I see, Josiah!"

All eyes went to the doorway where Joseph Putnam stood beaming at them.

"The boy is not to be trusted when it comes to food," he said as he strode into the room. "I'll wager he's got a few macaroons stuffed into his shirtsleeves even now. Those are his special favorite." He took hold of Josiah's arm and gently pried him away from the surprised Reverend Parris. "Shall I check inside his vest for you, Reverend?"

"He wasn't after food!" Nathaniel Ingersoll shouted. "He was after information!"

"Ah," said Joseph Putnam, his eyes shining, "and did he get any?"

"There was none to get!" Reverend Parris said. "I have nothing to hide from anyone."

"It's a good man, then," Joseph Putnam said, while Josiah watched his eyes flash at Reverend Parris like piercing points of light. "And you won't mind my taking young Hutchinson here with me, eh? I know how to deal with these food thieves."

With that, he slid Josiah smoothly past the table and out

the kitchen door into the hall. "Be off with you now," he whispered when they were safely out of earshot of the flustered Reverend Parris. "And stay out of the man's path."

But Josiah clutched at his sleeve. "Joseph, wait, please!"

Joseph leaned down. "What is it, Captain?"

Josiah opened his mouth to speak, but the words stuck in his throat. It couldn't possibly be true, could it? That Papa would plan with the Porters to take the church land away from Reverend Parris? And what if it were? Should he tell—on his own father?

Josiah swallowed hard and whispered, "Thank you, sir."

Joseph Putnam chuckled softly and caught Josiah's hand. He tucked something soft and warm into it. "Take this with you. Perhaps you can share it with your friends there, eh?"

Josiah looked first at the blueberry tart Joseph had slipped into his hand and then at the two wispy forms who watched them from the landing of the stairs.

"Josiah!" the taller form whispered. "Come here, quickly!"

☩ ⬧ ☩

Chapter Eleven

osiah took the stairs two at a time and once at the top followed Betty Parris around the corner and out of sight of the grown-ups below. Betty stopped and handed Dorcas to him, and the little girl nuzzled her face into his neck and sighed sleepily. Josiah shifted awkwardly as Betty tugged at his sleeve with butterfly fingers.

"Mama sent me up here to rest," she said, "and I heard the little angel whimpering, so I thought to bring her to you." There was a shiver in her voice as she added, "I have something to tell you!"

Josiah glanced over his shoulder and leaned in.

"'Tis Deliverance Carrier!" she murmured breathlessly. "I saw her!"

Josiah could feel his eyes widening in the darkness. "Where?" he said.

"I was out in the wagon with my father when he went to see Thomas Putnam—just yesterday—and I saw her lurking near that bog."

"Hathorne's Great Swamp?" Josiah said.

"Yes. She has long, stringy hair and a nose that nearly meets her chin, aye?"

Josiah nodded.

"She looked like a stray cat to me," Betty said.

"I have to find her and help her so she can keep Dorcas."

"Me," Dorcas murmured from his neck.

"Then you must find her," Betty said.

Josiah sighed heavily. "I don't know when, though. I'll be doin' more farmwork than ever now. I don't know how I can get leave to go searchin' for her."

"Aye," Betty said fiercely. She balled up her butterfly hands into fists. "I can't do anything without Abigail questionin' me like I was a criminal! But if I see the beggar woman again, I'll send you a message."

"Betty!" called a shrill voice from below.

Josiah stiffened and flattened himself against the wall.

"That's Papa!" she said.

"Then go!" Josiah said.

She blew a kiss to Dorcas and, gathering her black skirts about her, flitted down the stairs like a baby bird.

Josiah waited until he heard the front door slam and was sure the Parris family had left before he slid down the steps to search for Papa. He had to tell him about Deliverance.

The crowd had thinned out, and only a few men's voices drifted from the best room as Josiah skidded to a halt in the doorway. The heads of Papa, Benjamin, and Giles were bent over a piece of paper on the table, and none of them came up to spot him.

"I have heard of this agreement," Josiah's father said, "but

I didn't believe it ever actually existed."

"Aye, it did!" Giles sang out. "I was only able to get hold of it recently for Israel, and he bid me show it to you when he'd passed on. He said you'd know what to do about it."

Joseph Hutchinson raised his head and looked right into Giles Porter's eyes. "What do you mean, Giles?" he said.

Silently, Josiah backed out of the doorway and hurried down the hall. It was certain that at this moment, Papa had no time to listen to foggy information about Deliverance Carrier. Perhaps this was a job for the Merry Band.

He waited until the house was silent that night before he leaned toward Hope's bed and hissed, "Are you awake?"

The curtain parted a crack. "Aye, what is it? And don't wake up this baby."

"Her mother's still around the village."

Hope yanked the curtains back and stared at him. "Are you certain?"

"Aye, someone saw her."

"Who?"

"It doesn't matter—"

"*Who?*"

Josiah sighed. "Betty Parris."

"I told you, you cannot trust any of those people!" Hope whispered hoarsely.

Josiah could hear the fear climbing up her throat. "All right, forget about Betty, then," he said. "But we can still find Deliverance—the Merry Band can."

"There is no Merry Band anymore."

"Aye, there is! We don't need Rachel and Ezekiel!"

"We need to stay home where it's safe!"

"We need to find Dorcas's mother!"

"Then you'll do it without me!" she cried, and she snapped the curtains shut.

It was still in the room, and Josiah was sure he'd never felt more alone. He'd prayed to God that he could find Deliverance Carrier, and God finally seemed to be answering. But what was he supposed to do now?

Papa was involved in his own serious problems—things Josiah wasn't sure he wanted to know about.

Hope was so frightened of who-knows-what that she wanted no part in any plan.

That left only William and Sarah in the Merry Band, and Sarah was too much of a rabbit to be of help.

Maybe it was time anyway—time to be a man and act alone. *That's what I'll do*, he thought as he huddled under his quilt.

But that was easier to say than to do. Papa spent more time than ever with Benjamin Porter, sorting out the business of the sawmill, and more and more of the farmwork fell to Josiah. But as he went about his chores, with Dorcas always at his heels, he formed a plan in his mind.

The next step was going to be a hard one, but it had to be done. The Putnams were the only people he hadn't asked, and surely one of them had seen her lurking about. Now Josiah just had to wait for his chance to slip away to do it— and it came in the most peculiar way.

He was chopping wood for the supper fire a few days later when Mama poked her head out the back door.

"Josiah," she said, "I've just found this note hanging from the knocker. Will you be my eyes for me?"

Josiah wiped his hands on his breeches and reached for the rolled-up piece of parchment. Most of the women in Salem Village couldn't read or write. Since he'd learned, Mama had come to depend on him "to be her eyes," as she always put it.

The writing on the paper was round and careful. Some of the words were spelled differently than he had ever seen them, but the message was clear: "Please send Josiah to Josef Putnams at wons," Josiah read the note aloud to his mother. "Important."

"'Tis curious Joseph didn't simply come here himself," Mama said.

Josiah studied the letters again. This note hadn't been written by his teacher. Joseph Putnam's handwriting was bold, and the words always finished in big flourishes that Josiah had tried to copy and never could. Perhaps Joseph's young wife, Constance, had written this. Did that mean something was wrong with Joseph? Josiah looked up quickly at his mother.

"May I go now?" he said.

"I suppose you must," Mama said, "as soon as you've brought in enough wood for the supper—"

But Josiah was already out the door and swinging his ax before she could finish the sentence. Within 10 minutes, he was racing across Wolf Pits Meadow, his thoughts tangled in his head. *What could be so important that Joseph would send for him during the day, when he knew he was working for Papa? Was he so ill that he had to have Constance write for him? What was he going to find when he got there?*

What he found when he reached the elegant white house

was Joseph Putnam himself sitting on his front porch frown-
ing over a stack of serious-looking papers. His face broke into
a grin when he saw Josiah pounding across the yard.

"Captain! To what do I owe this visit? I thought you'd be
laboring in the fields!"

Josiah screeched to a halt on the top step and gulped for
breath. Joseph's grin dissolved, and he put his papers aside.

"What is it, son? Is there trouble?"

"No," Josiah said. "I came because—didn't you send
for me?"

"I?" said Joseph Putnam. His eyebrows shot up. "Send for
you how?"

Josiah fumbled with his whistle pouch and brought out
the crumpled note. Joseph studied it for a moment, and when
he looked up, his eyes were twinkling. "Did you think I wrote
this, Captain?"

"Well, no, sir," Josiah stammered. "But I thought perhaps
Constance—"

"Constance can think of nothing but knitting little boots
no bigger than your heel," Joseph said, chuckling. "There's to
be a new Putnam before the summer's over, if you'll recall."
He handed the message back to Josiah. "I think someone has
played a prank on us both, Captain. And from the looks of it,
she's not much older than that little babe you've been toting
about on your shoulders of late."

"She?" Josiah said.

"Aye, it's sure that's a girl's pen we're seeing there." His
eyes crackled merrily. "A boy would have at least one ink blot
on a message of that length, eh?"

Josiah nodded quickly and stuffed the note back into his

whistle pouch. His thoughts were racing, and he backed toward the steps.

"I'd best be gone, then," he said.

"Then you won't be staying for some tea?" Joseph said.

Josiah just shook his head and scrambled down the steps.

"Good day, then, Captain!" Joseph called to him.

But Josiah just waved as he made for Hathorne's Hill. There could be only one girl who would send him a message to get him away from the farm in the middle of the day. Betty Parris had bought him some time, but only a little. If he were going to question the Putnams, he had to do it in a hurry.

He didn't have time to be afraid until he'd already let the knocker on Thomas Putnam's door clatter and was catching his breath on the top step. By then it was too late to change his mind. Ann Putnam Jr. opened the door almost at once. Her eyes glittered when she saw him. The only business he had ever had with Ann had been last summer, and it had left her hating him more than ever.

"What is it, boy?" she said. Her voice always made Josiah think a spider must talk the way she did. She pushed back a piece of thin hair that wouldn't stay under her cap and sighed impatiently. "Abigail is right. You are a brainless boy. If you've something to ask, then ask it."

The hair on the back of Josiah's neck bristled. He took a deep breath. "I thought to ask if you've had any beggars at your door of late."

Ann's suspicious eyes slanted down at him. "Why?" she said.

Josiah slanted his eyes back at her. "Well," he said slyly,

"we mustn't have the likes of them lurking about our doors, must we? I thought to run her off."

"Who?"

"Deliverance Carrier. She's the worst of them, you know."

Ann leaned in, her eyes aglow with interest. "Has she a long nose, like a witch, and the smell of a dead rat about her?"

"Aye!"

"Why, she was in the woods—"

"Shut it, Ann! Tell this boy nothing!" a stern voice said from behind the door.

They both turned as Ann Putnam Sr. appeared in the doorway beside her daughter. Her sleeves were rolled up and several spikes of hair stood straight out from under her cap.

"He was askin' about that wretched beggar woman," young Ann cried. "He thinks to run her off!"

"He thinks nothing of the kind!" said her mother. "The Hutchinsons are forever preachin' how we should take pity on such people." Goody Putnam's small eyes aimed at Josiah like two pieces of buckshot. "Your papa thinks he's so high and mighty with his new wealth and his Salem Town connections. He even thinks he's too good for Reverend Parris. But I'll tell you something, boy." She leveled a thin finger at Josiah. "All this kindness he shows to beggars and others who are not of our faith—he'll have to answer for that on the Judgment Day! And in the meantime, he'll get no friendship from the Putnams!"

With that, she slammed the heavy door, and Josiah was left standing on the stoop with the startled clatter of the knocker ringing in his ears. That was that, then. *I was a brainless boy*, Josiah thought, *to think any Putnam other than*

Joseph would ever help a Hutchinson—or anyone else for that matter!

Puffing up air that sent the curls on his forehead dancing, Josiah turned to go. He hadn't taken one step when he was suddenly flying through the air with a pair of wiry arms clamped around his middle.

"I've got you now, boy!" a voice snarled in his ear. "I've got you now."

✝ ✛ ✝

Chapter Twelve

osiah felt the ground pass roughly beneath him as he was dragged away from the Putnam house. Before he could catch his breath to try to squirm away, another pair of hands joined the first, and he was lifted by the armpits and carried in the direction of Hathorne's Great Swamp.

"What are you about here, boy?" Richard Putnam hissed in one ear.

"Whatever it is, it was a stupid errand, eh?" Jonathon hissed in the other.

"Let me go!" Josiah screamed at them. "I've as much right to walk the streets of Essex County as you!"

"You aren't walking the streets," Richard said, gripping his prisoner's arm until Josiah was sure he'd squeeze it off. "You're walking Putnam property!"

"What have you there?" another voice called. Richard and Jonathon didn't stop dragging Josiah toward the swamp, but Richard did toss his head backward to call out to his cousin Eleazer, "A brainless boy!"

"More brainless than ever!" Jonathon said. "Walking across our land in broad daylight."

"It isn't your land!" Josiah said to him. "You live clear over on the other side of the village!"

Jonathon jerked to a halt and pulled Josiah away from Richard, close to his bulging eyes. "Putnam land is Putnam land," he hissed. His breath was hot and smelled of onions. "Whether it belongs to my father or one of my uncles makes no difference. You're trespassing, and you'll pay."

"Come on, Jonathon," Richard said. "Let's get him to the swamp."

He cupped his hand around Josiah's arm again, and once more they half-dragged, half-carried him toward the bog. Josiah could hear Eleazer buzzing behind them like an annoying fly.

"What are we going to do with him at the swamp?" he said with relish in his voice.

"First, we'll make him talk," Richard said. "Eh, Jonathon? We'll make him tell us what he's really doing here."

"How will we do it?" Eleazer cried. Even as Josiah kicked his feet and fought to get away, he could hear Eleazer licking his chops in anticipation. "Too bad you don't have your knife this time." He cackled gleefully. "Remember what we did to his sister?"

Jonathon stopped so short that Josiah was jerked from his grasp and landed in a sprawl at their feet.

"Shut it, idiot!" Jonathon screeched at his cousin. "You're an idiot!"

For a fleeting moment, Josiah watched as Jonathon pulled back his hand and let it fly straight at Eleazer's face. Richard, too, raised his fist at the boy in anger, but Josiah didn't wait to see where it would connect. Scrambling to his feet, he tore toward the swamp.

"He's getting away!" one of them cried.

But before they could even start for him, Josiah veered to the east and sailed toward Joseph Putnam's house. His heart nearly sprang out of his mouth when he saw his teacher standing on the porch, squinting at him through the sunlight. As he ran, he sneaked a glance over his shoulder. Jonathon and Richard had stopped short at the sight of their half uncle and stood, fists doubled, at the edge of his property.

"Ahoy there, Captain!" Joseph called out to Josiah. "Two visits in one day?"

Josiah clambered up the steps and looked behind him again. Jonathon and Richard had disappeared. Eleazer was probably still lying on the ground groaning, if he was conscious at all.

"No, sir," Josiah said, panting like a charging bull as he gripped the porch railing. "I . . . must . . . to home."

Joseph Putnam placed his fingers under his chin like a pistol and watched Josiah carefully. "You're all right?" he said.

Josiah could only nod.

"Get you home, and tell your mother the message I sent was a false alarm."

Josiah looked up quickly. Joseph chuckled softly. "I'm a nervous new father—I know nothing of these things. Tell her I thought Constance's time had come, but alas, we have months to go yet, eh?"

Josiah stared at him.

"Let you tell her that," Joseph said, "and then let you be

careful where these secret messages lead you. I fear the Putnam boys no longer play boyish games."

The spring night was warm, and long after Hope and Dorcas had gone to sleep, Josiah got up from his cot and padded softly to the window. He sat on the blanket trunk that stood under the sill and looked down over Salem Village.

It was so peaceful tonight, with just a wispy breeze moving the new leaves and a bit of moonlight peeking through them.

How can any place so peaceful hold so much danger? he wondered.

Hope had been right. The Putnams were more dangerous than they had ever imagined. As he reviewed the day in his mind—the way he did so often at night—he saw nothing but their treachery.

Eleazer had said, "Too bad you don't have your knife. Remember what we did to his sister?"

Even the day Nathaniel Putnam had pulled out his musket and stuck it into Papa's face—and Jonathon himself had held his knife threateningly against his sleeve as he'd looked at Josiah—Josiah had thought the Putnams were all bluster and empty threats. Josiah had always been afraid of them, but a knife—that was a weapon. That wasn't something you used for a prank.

Josiah looked back at the curtains that shielded his sister's bed. The last day Hope had seemed like a girl to him—instead of a pinched, frightened old woman—was the day the Putnams had chased her up Hathorne's Hill. She had never told him what had happened, but she'd been terrified ever since. "Remember what we did to his sister?" Eleazer had said. What did he mean? Did it have something to do with the knife?

Josiah turned to the window and looked at the village again. It was sure he wouldn't be asking her. If he brought it up, she'd only want to know how he'd found out. He surely wasn't going to tell her what had happened to him today. She'd be more terrified than ever.

Josiah shook his head. He'd already asked God to help him, and it looked as if his prayers were working. Maybe God was getting closer. Maybe.

On the east side of the Hutchinsons' land, just along a branch of Crane Brook, lay the only marshland on their property. But Joseph Hutchinson had even made good use of that. He planted grass there that he harvested every summer to feed the cattle. Josiah was tossing seeds into the swamp the next day when he heard a hissing from the brush.

"Psst!"

At first, no one seemed to be there. But then something moved at the edge of the brush—something black that said again, "Pssst!"

It was Tituba, Reverend Parris's slave. Josiah sloshed his way toward her, and she shrank back into the brush.

"Do you want me?" Josiah said.

"Shhh!" she said in a violent whisper. "We don't want nobody hear us."

Josiah crouched down next to her. "What is it?" he said.

"Dis for you," she answered. She pressed her warm, black hand into his and pulled it away, leaving a neatly folded piece of parchment in his palm.

Josiah could feel his pulse racing. "Is this from Betty?"

"You don' tell *nobody!*" Tituba said. Her black eyes flashed with fear. "I no want me Betty get in trouble!"

"I won't tell anybody," Josiah said solemnly.

Tituba looked nervously over her shoulder. "You go now," she said. "You go!"

But before he could even turn around, Tituba had gathered her muddy skirts around her and was gone. Josiah stayed crouched in the underbrush and unfolded the paper.

Reverend Parris can't be too bad off, he thought. Very few people in Salem Village could afford the luxury of paper. Even Josiah's papa wrote messages on thin pieces of bark.

But as Josiah read the words that were written so carefully in Betty Parris's round hand, it wouldn't have mattered if it had been carved into a piece of bear skin. "I no werr the littul gurls mama is," it said. "She has a leen-to at the edj of the marsh on the morning sun side of thorndik Hil. Be kerful."

A lean-to—that had to be some kind of shelter Deliverance had built for herself. The edge of a marsh would be pretty wet, Josiah thought as he looked down at his own soaked breeches. But then, no one would think to look for her there.

Josiah studied the note again. On the morning sun side of Thorndike Hill. The east. That was certainly away from people. But whose property was it on?

Josiah's head came up from the paper like a snapping whip.

That was Nathaniel Putnam's land! Papa had pointed it out to him the day they had beaten the bounds. It was one of many spots the Putnams owned that couldn't be farmed.

Josiah crammed the note into his whistle pouch and snatched up the now-empty seed bag. Even if he couldn't get Deliverance to come and get Dorcas, at least he could warn her that she was in danger if Nathaniel Putnam found her on his land. He had to get to her before Nathaniel did.

But almost before his feet began to run, they slowed to a stop. If Nathaniel Putnam found anybody on his land who wasn't supposed to be there, he would probably be looking down the barrel of his musket.

I can't do this alone, Josiah thought wildly. *But who would go with me?*

William Proctor was too far away, and Josiah had to get there fast. Joseph Putnam would tell him it was too dangerous and insist he tell his father. But Papa had enough to worry about right now. If only . . .

Josiah looked longingly across Crane Brook toward Ipswich Road. It was only a five-minute run from here to Ezekiel's.

Josiah stuffed the empty seed bag into the waist of his breeches and took off at a gallop toward the Porter farm. He was only halfway across the front yard when Ezekiel came around from the back of the house to meet him.

"What do you want?" he said. His voice was stiff. "Is somebody chasing you?"

"Nay, well, not yet." Josiah gasped for air and tried to choose his words. "I know where Deliverance Carrier is. I need to get to her. She's on Putnam land."

Ezekiel's already huge eyes widened. "They'll have her thrown in jail or worse."

"Aye, but I have to find her, and I need someone to help me."

Ezekiel's skin seemed to pinch over his sharp Porter cheekbones. "You're asking me to go with you?"

"Aye, you said you wanted to prove to me you were no coward. Here's your chance."

Ezekiel chewed on the inside of his mouth. "How did you find out where the old woman is?"

"Betty Parris saw her. She sent me a message."

Ezekiel's eyebrows shot up. "Betty Parris! I said I was no coward. I'm not stupid either!"

Josiah could feel his cheeks beginning to burn. "I should have known you'd find an excuse, Ezekiel Porter!" he cried. "Every time a friend needs you, you find some reason to run away!"

"It's a pretty good reason, don't you think?" Ezekiel shouted back. "You can't trust a Parris. They're all in league with the Putnams. For all you know, it's a trap you're walkin' into!"

"That's the way rabbits think!" Josiah hurled the words angrily over his shoulder as he turned to go. "You're nothing but a frightened rabbit, Ezekiel Porter, and you always will be!"

"You're a foolish boy, Josiah Hutchinson!" Ezekiel howled from behind him. But Josiah could barely hear him. He was already halfway home.

By the time Josiah reached the Hutchinson farm, the anger had died down inside him and there was only fear left. Walking into the house, he thought, *What am I going to do now?* Dorcas's mother was right there in Nathaniel Putnam's backyard, and no one would help him find her.

There was only one thing to do—go to Nathaniel Putnam's himself. *That's what a man would do*, Josiah thought miserably. *But who am I fooling? I am as much a coward as Ezekiel Porter.*

Shoulders sagging, he went to the window. He could see his mother's and Hope's white caps, looking like dots from here as they weeded the onion field. That was an all-day job, so they must have Dorcas with them, though he couldn't see her. She was probably chirping away, thinking any minute her mother was going to come back and get her.

Josiah brought up his chin. *You* are *a coward, Josiah Hutchinson*, he said to himself. *Why don't you just sneak to the Putnams', warn Deliverance Carrier, and run back here? You've always been faster than any of them.*

"But they're more dangerous than we ever thought," he could hear Hope say.

"The Putnam boys no longer play boyish games," Joseph Putnam's voice joined in.

Josiah brought his head up and grabbed the seed bag from the waistband of his breeches. Even if Deliverance wouldn't come back with him, he could tell her to move to a safer place and give her some food to hold her over until Papa could decide what was to be done for her. As he shoved the remains of the bread from dinner, a few carrots, and some beef jerky into the bag, his eyes darted to the window. The white caps looked farther away than ever. He'd be back before they even finished the weeding.

"We'll see who's a coward, Ezekiel Porter," Josiah muttered as he tucked the bag of food inside his shirt and went for the door. "And we'll see who's a man."

Josiah was about to cross the road when he heard his front door slam shut. He whirled around to see Dorcas standing forlornly on the stoop.

"'Siah!" her tiny voice chirped.

Josiah ran back toward the house, and Dorcas toddled to him. Her eyes blinked sleepily up into the sun. The crease of the pillow was still on her cheek.

"They left you upstairs to nap?" Josiah said.

Instead of answering, she held her arms in the air to be picked up.

Josiah squinted toward the onion field. Hope or Mama would be coming back to check on her soon. "Go back upstairs, Dorcas," Josiah said. "Go back to sleep."

But Dorcas's face puckered and she tugged at his shirt. Josiah looked up at the sun. Time was getting away.

"All right, then," he said quickly. He pulled Dorcas onto his back, and the giggles squeezed out of her like bubbles from a soapy tub. "But hold on tight. We must be back before they discover you're gone."

✠ ✠ ✠

etty Parris had been right. At the edge of the stretch of marshland on Nathaniel Putnam's property lay several rotting slabs of wood supported by a large rock and sheltered on either side by layers of rushes and cattails. Josiah knew if he hadn't been looking for the lean-to, he would have passed it by as a pile of trash left by some careless Putnam.

"That's your mama's house," Josiah whispered to Dorcas.

"Mama?" she chirped.

"Shhh! Let's see if she's home."

Josiah set Dorcas on the ground and led her toward the pitiful little hut. But when he peeked in, there was nothing inside but a piece of old rag.

Dorcas crawled to it and clutched it in her hand.

"Mama?" she said again. This time her voice was sad, and tiny tears sparkled in her eyes.

That's a piece of Deliverance's skirt, Josiah said to himself. *Where is she with the rest of it?* His thoughts raced, but he forced himself to sit next to Dorcas and smile.

"Perhaps she'll be back soon," he said. "We'll wait for her."

But Dorcas crawled to the small opening and whimpered. Fitfully, she pointed out of the lean-to.

"Here!" Josiah said suddenly. "You can play with this." He fumbled to get his whistle pouch off and dangled it in front of her. The dimples appeared in her cheeks, and Josiah noticed how round and rosy they were looking. Even the two hands that came up to bat at the pouch were plump and pink now.

She chirped happily as her fingers curled around the pouch, and she snuggled down with her head in his lap to play with it.

I wish it were that easy to forget all my problems, Josiah thought as he watched her drift off to sleep. *I wish I had somebody to come in and take it all away—or at least tell me what to do.*

He tried to straighten his shoulders and think like the man he was attempting to be. *I know Papa never feels like this,* he thought. *He always knows what to do, but who tells him?*

"Aye, here's a footprint in the mud!" a voice hissed from outside.

Josiah stiffened and listened.

"Here's another one!"

"He was heading right for your father's property!"

"This *is* my father's property, idiot!"

That could only be Jonathon Putnam's voice. Josiah curled in a ball over Dorcas. Perhaps if he were completely quiet, they would pass right by as he almost had.

"Here's yet another footprint!" he heard Eleazer whisper loudly.

Josiah looked down at his boots. The soles were caked with mud. His footprints were leading them straight to him. Easing out from under Dorcas's head, Josiah slid through the opening and out of the lean-to. If he could just draw them away from here, he could come back for Dorcas before she woke up. Some snapping twigs would pull them toward—

"Well, well, what have we here?" said Jonathon Putnam.

Josiah looked up—into the flashing eyes of the Putnam cousins. Jonathon and Eleazer hauled him to his feet.

"It's nothing but the village idiot," Jonathon said.

Eleazer snorted triumphantly. "Aye, so it is!"

Josiah tried to pull away, but Jonathon had his arms pulled firmly behind his back. There was nowhere to run anyway. Richard Putnam stood squarely in front of him, and one glance over his shoulder revealed Silas at his back.

"You got away from us the other day," Jonathon said, tightening his wiry grip around Josiah's wrists.

"Ran to our sissy uncle, you did!" Eleazer cried. "But if we'd had our knife . . . if we hadn't lost it—"

"Shut it!" Jonathon's voice spat at his cousin. "It was your idiotic jabbering that let him escape last time. I can take him without a knife. Now shut it!"

Eleazer followed orders, and Jonathon turned his attention to his other two cousins. "What will it be, gentlemen? A swim in the Frost Fish River? Or perhaps a swing from a tree in yonder woods?"

Josiah's mind was racing. He had to get them away from here before Dorcas woke up.

"I'd prefer to swim," he said suddenly, "if I were to have a choice."

"Then a tree it is!" Jonathon cried.

With a heave, he hoisted Josiah over one wiry shoulder and took off at a trot. Josiah strained his ears to listen for cries from Dorcas, but all he could hear were the shouts of the Putnam boys as they hauled him toward Thorndike Hill.

"Have you got them tight?" Jonathon said.

"Aye," Richard answered. "He won't be working his way out of those knots."

Josiah yanked his hands against the ropes that cut into his wrists.

"See?" Eleazer shouted. "He can't move at all!"

Silas pulled a piece of cloth across his eyes and another over his mouth, and Josiah could feel him tying both at the back of his head. A few moments later, someone else bound his feet and yanked him with more ropes around his chest, tying him tightly to a tree.

"Good, then," Jonathon said. "It's sure he won't be marching across Putnam land anymore."

"When will we untie him?" Eleazer said.

"Don't be a fool! We've naught to untie him at all. Let someone else do it."

"Like who?" Silas asked, and Josiah could hear the caution in his voice.

"Like . . . anyone. A bear, perhaps?"

There was a round of laughter, and Josiah held his breath to keep from tugging at the ropes in a panic.

"Good day, then, village idiot," Jonathon said. "You won't get away like your smart sister did. Come along, gentlemen."

There was a chorus of rough laughing and sharp-edged

good-byes. At last, the stand of trees at the base of Thorndike Hill was quiet. But Josiah's mind was alive with shouting. *What did you do to my sister?* it cried. *You tied her up, too?* And then his thoughts centered like a pointing finger. "If we had our knife ...," Eleazer had said. "Remember what we did to his sister?"

A picture formed in Josiah's mind that made him writhe and strain against the ropes like a tethered calf. Being tied up would only make Hope angry. It was sure at least one of the Putnams had ended up with teeth marks in his arm.

But to have a knife held to her throat when she could do nothing to save herself, that would put the terror in anyone's eyes. Even Hope's.

Twisting like a madman going to the stocks, Josiah fought against the ropes. But Richard Putnam had been right—he couldn't work his way out of the knots.

If I could get a rock to cut the ropes, he thought frantically. But the only part of him he could move were his legs, and scraping them over the ground didn't turn up a single stone. *How would I grab hold of it anyway?*

His mind spun, and he bit his lip to keep from crying. He knew it would be dark soon. Dorcas would wake up terrified. Who would be there to hear her except maybe another Putnam? Why had he brought Dorcas along? It was bad enough that he was bear bait, but a helpless little girl who trusted him. . . .

Suddenly, Josiah caught his breath. *What was that?*

It came again—a rustling from deep in the woods. *It's nothing*, Josiah told himself wildly. *It's naught but the leaves blowing.*

But the rustling grew louder, and with it the crashing of footsteps amid the twigs and underbrush.

It's a bear! Josiah's mind screamed at him. *It's a bear, and I'm about to be eaten.*

The hurried, unsteady footsteps were only a few strides away when they stopped. There was no other sound—except the startled cry of a woman.

"What are ye . . . ? Yer tied up like a bundle of hay!"

Josiah chewed at the gag, but a pair of clawed hands pulled it off and then the blindfold.

Deliverance peered at him through the panels of colorless hair that hung over her eyes. "Who done this to ye?" she said.

"It doesn't matter! Untie my hands. Please, we have to get to Dorcas!"

"Dorcas?" Her claws froze over the ropes, and she brought her pointed chin close to his face.

"She's sleeping in your lean-to," Josiah said. "I had to leave her there so they wouldn't find her."

Deliverance dropped the ropes she had just removed from his hands and feet and took off toward Putnam land.

"Wait!" Josiah cried in a loud whisper. But she didn't. He stumbled after her.

The evening was a heavy gray around him as he crashed through the trees. With a lurch, he charged into Deliverance's back. She stood stone-still at the edge of the woods.

"Come on. It's that way!" Josiah said.

But she didn't move. Instead, she whirled around to look behind them both, and one of her clawed hands dug into Josiah's arm. At their backs, a rustling in the trees sent a chill up Josiah's spine.

He'd only heard that rustling once before. This time he wasn't mistaken.

Out of the trees lumbered a sniffing, panting bear.

☩ ⋆☩⋆ ☩

Chapter Fourteen

Deliverance Carrier's fingers dug hard into Josiah's arm. The rest of her body was frozen against him.

For a moment, Josiah was paralyzed, too. Even his thoughts were motionless as he stared in horror at the bear.

The big animal had emerged through the trees on all fours like a huge, clumsy baby. Now he stood up on his hind legs, the top of his head brushing the tree branches. With several powerful grunts, he sniffed the air.

Josiah's thoughts jarred loose. *He's hungry. He smells food. He smells us.*

The bear pulled a paw across his chest and scratched. Even in the near dark, Josiah could see his claws, longer than his own fingers, and a shiver of fear shook through him.

Savagely, the big animal raked his nails across his massive front, while Josiah's eyes followed them back and forth in terror. Any minute, those same talons could be tearing into his flesh and Deliverance's. He had to *do* something.

If they ran, the bear would scoop them up like so many

beetles. If they stayed, he would sniff them out and snatch them up with the same claws that were this minute scraping across his hairy skin.

Josiah's hand went to his own chest, and he clutched his shirt to keep his heart from pounding out onto the ground. If he didn't do something fast, he was sure the bear would hear it and rip it from his—

But Josiah's terrified thoughts fell over each other and stopped as his hand groped at something bulky—there, under his shirt.

It was the seed bag, full of the food he had brought for Deliverance.

Food. That's what the bear was looking for, and Josiah was carrying a whole sack of it. But could he get the bear to take it—and not the two of them?

Quietly, hardly daring to move at all, Josiah reached inside his shirt and slowly started pulling out the bag. He had to get it out there on the ground, where the bear would see it before he spotted them. Once he was distracted by carrots and beef jerky, they could slip away. But he knew they had to be absolutely silent—or they would be beef jerky themselves.

Inch by inch, the bag emerged from under Josiah's shirt. It seemed the harder he tugged, the harder the bear snorted at the air, but still he didn't turn his eyes their way. Just a little more and he could have the bear's supper right at his feet.

Suddenly, with a grunt they could have heard back at the Hutchinson farm, the bear turned to the tree and laid the bark open with one swipe of his frustrated paw. This was his chance, Josiah knew. Sucking in air, he yanked the seed bag all the way out of his shirt and crouched close to the ground.

With the bear turned away, making all that racket, he could step just a little closer and get the food where the bear couldn't miss it.

The big animal groaned and pulled his shiny nails down the tree, tearing more bark away. Josiah clutched the bag and inched forward.

"No, boy!" Deliverance burst out beside him. "No!"

With one jerk of his head, the bear had his eyes on Josiah. They gleamed meanly in the dark. For an instant, Josiah froze. It was over. He was going to die—ripped to shreds by the claws that now tore at the air above him. Josiah couldn't move.

Behind him there was a whimper. For a second, Josiah thought it was Dorcas, until another set of claws dug at his sleeve. Deliverance Carrier was clinging to him, crying like a child.

Josiah's mind went into motion again. With a heave, he tossed the seed bag full of food at the bear's feet.

The bear's eyes glittered suspiciously down at it, but he remained still for what seemed like longer than one of Reverend Parris's sermons. Josiah squeezed his eyes shut. *Please, God, let him pick it up—before Deliverance screams again.*

When Josiah opened his eyes, the bear was still staring at the bag, but he began to sniff again. His big snorts were rewarded with the scent of beef jerky, and his paw swiped down to pick it up. He sniffed at it and opened his mouth to comment. Josiah was so close he could smell the bear's foul breath—and see his long, yellow teeth.

Josiah took two careful steps backward, with Deliverance still clinging desperately to his sleeve. The bear didn't even glitter his eyes over them again. He ripped open the bag, and his entire head disappeared inside.

"Let's go!" Josiah hissed, and they turned and fled from the woods. Branches slapped their faces and twigs slashed at their arms as the trees whipped by in a blur. Josiah could feel Deliverance's nails digging into his flesh, but he dragged her with him as his feet pumped over the wet ground toward the edge of the woods, toward Dorcas.

"This way," he commanded, and veered sharply to the left.

But Goody Carrier's feet slid crazily through the mud and flew out from under her tattered skirts. Still clutching at Josiah's shirt, she pulled him down on top of her.

"Get up, boy!" she cried. "Get up!"

"Shhh!" Josiah's head came up, and he cocked it to listen. Behind them, the trees crashed against each other.

"Dear Lord, protect us," Deliverance whispered. Her voice cracked into a dry whimper.

But Josiah still listened. "He's going the other way," he whispered back.

They lay in the mud in silence until the last leaf had stopped rustling. Then Deliverance poked a bony finger into Josiah's chest.

"Yer crushin' me, boy," she said.

Josiah scrambled off of her, and she sat up and peered at him in the dark.

"Was that some spell you cast back there?" she said.

"No! 'Twas food. Beef jerky and a crust of bread. I . . . I brought it for you."

"A good thing it is ye didn't offer it to me sooner, or we'd have been no better'n a crust of bread ourselves." She looked at him curiously. "Yer an odd sort of boy, ye are. And a whole lot smarter'n ye look."

Josiah wasn't sure that was a compliment, and he didn't care. He'd started to shake, and he was sure any minute he was going to throw up in the mud.

But suddenly, Goody Carrier stood up on her spindly legs. "I've got to get to Dorcas," she said.

"Wait!" Josiah said.

"For what!" she snapped over her shoulder. "My child's in the dark alone!"

"It's Putnam land you built your shelter on," Josiah said. "If we're caught, we'll all land in jail—Dorcas, too."

Deliverance stopped, and her eyes squinted at him.

"Please, let's go to my father," he said. "He'll know what to do."

But Deliverance shook her head and turned to go again. "Not before I find my child. It's one thing leavin' her with people I thought I could trust and another leavin' her out here with who-knows-what comin' after her."

She tottered a few steps and careened toward the ground, her arms flailing. Josiah caught one bony wrist in his hand.

"All right. Come on, then," he said. "Follow me. And stay quiet. The Putnams will be listening for us, surely."

He didn't wait for her to agree, but scrambled into the underbrush that bordered the creek. If they crawled silently, they would come out just before the marsh without being discovered.

It was completely dark when they reached the lean-to. Deliverance got to her feet and hobbled hurriedly to the little shack. Before Josiah could get there, she had crawled out again. Even in the inky night, Josiah could tell what was written on her face. Dorcas wasn't there.

Suddenly, Josiah didn't care whether a thousand Putnams heard him. "Dorcas!" he shouted frantically. "Dorcas, where are you?"

Deliverance added her brittle voice, and they both called until Josiah's words grew raspy and the beggar woman had to sit to catch her breath. Her face was gray and drawn into a knot.

"I've naught to do but wait for her," she said in a thin voice.

"I'll search the—"

"No." Her bony hand caught his arm. "Ye do what ye said before. Go to yer father. He'll know what to do."

Because once again I don't, Josiah finished for her.

There wasn't a star in the sky as Josiah made his way home, still looking fearfully over his shoulder. He tried not to think of how frightened little Dorcas must be, wherever she was.

"Psst!" hissed a voice. "Hey, boy."

Josiah slowed his steps.

The hiss came again, and, glancing anxiously toward his house, Josiah stepped to the bushes that bordered the Meeting House property.

Tituba's black eyes shone at him in the darkness.

"Have you another message from Betty?" Josiah stuck out his hand.

"No paper," she said softly. "Me Betty, she say tell you— she have da little chile."

Josiah gasped. "Betty has Dorcas, the little girl I brought to the parsonage?"

"Yes, she have."

Josiah sucked in more air. "Does . . . does Reverend Parris know?" For the first time, Josiah could make out Tituba's whole face in the inky darkness. Her cheeks were pinched in fear.

"Yes, he know," she said. Her voice trembled. "Mr. Thomas Putnam bring to the door, right to the door—"

Josiah didn't wait to hear more. "Tell Betty I'll be back for Dorcas," he called over his shoulder. "I'll bring my father."

And then he ran through the night toward the lights of the Hutchinson house.

When Josiah burst into the kitchen, Joseph Hutchinson stood up. The tired lines on his face seemed to crack open when he spoke.

"Where have you been, boy?"

"I . . . I'm sorry, sir. I was looking for Deliverance."

"Is Dorcas not with you?" his mother said.

Josiah shook his head. "No. But I know where she is— and Deliverance, too."

"Speak up, then," Papa said. "Where is the child?"

"Reverend Parris has her, sir. Thomas Putnam found her and took her there."

Papa's face clouded over. "How on earth . . . ?"

"Please, we have to get her away from them!"

Everyone's eyes turned to the corner. For the first time, Josiah saw Hope there. She was standing up, clenching a needle in her hand, her quilt forgotten at her feet. "Please, Papa, you must get her away from those people! Please, they'll hurt her!"

Joseph Hutchinson's eyes rested on Hope's ash-colored face for only a moment before he nodded. "I'll go to the parsonage," he said. "And Josiah, you'll come along with me. Perhaps you can untangle some of this madness as we go." There was anger in his voice, and Josiah knew he had put him in a place where he didn't want to be.

Josiah got only part of the story out before they reached the parsonage. There wasn't a light to be seen, and all the shutters were drawn and latched in the mild spring evening, as if in terror of some icy winter storm.

"The man's gone mad with his fears," Papa muttered as he knocked.

They heard a heavy bolt being moved back before the door came open. Abigail Williams stood for a second, smiling smugly down at Josiah, until Reverend Parris came up behind her.

"I didn't think it would be long before you came along, Hutchinson," he said in his tight whine. "But the woman isn't here."

Joseph Hutchinson blinked into the dim light that filtered forlornly out the door. "The woman?" he said.

"The beggar, the Carrier woman!" Reverend Parris said impatiently. "Nathaniel Putnam caught her on his property. Set up housekeeping in some makeshift hut, she did! Ezekiel Cheever's holding her at Ingersoll's Inn until she can be taken to the Salem Town jail."

"Where is the child?" Papa said.

"I don't know what you mean!"

"Do not dissemble with me, Mr. Parris!" Papa said through his teeth.

Josiah didn't know what *dissemble* meant, but it was clear Reverend Parris did. Although he drew himself up proudly, his lower lip trembled as he said, "Abigail, bring the child here."

"You had no need to send the child's mother off to jail, Mr. Parris," Goodman Hutchinson said. "She was only looking for food to stay alive."

The minister gave a hard laugh. "'Tis a poor mother indeed to leave her child wandering around in the woods at night."

Betty appeared in the doorway. Dorcas was clinging to her neck.

"'Siah!" Dorcas said with a whimper. She held out both little hands toward him.

"If you think you are going to take this child, Mr. Hutchinson, think again," Reverend Parris said. "She is part of Thomas Putnam's case against the Carrier woman. He'll be representing his brother."

"His case?" Papa thundered. "Thomas Putnam is a proper lawyer now, eh? Making cases against poor women who ask only to be given a crust of bread that he'd sooner give to one of his pigs?" Joseph Hutchinson gave an angry snort. "Go on and take the child, Josiah."

Dorcas was already straining toward him and starting to cry as Josiah reached for her. She flung her arms around him and clung hard.

"It's all right, little angel," Betty murmured.

"I demand to know what action you intend to take, Hutchinson," Reverend Parris shouted.

"I am under no bond to tell you what I intend, Mr. Parris."

The minister narrowed his eyes until Josiah thought they

would cross. "In spite of your carryings-on with the likes of Israel Porter, I thought you to be a man of God. I never truly thought you'd take part in the scheme to run me out of this church. But you've shown me now, mister."

"What nonsense is this?" Papa said.

"I know there's a plot afoot. I'm not a stupid man, you know."

"Oh, certainly not."

Papa was staring hard at Reverend Parris.

"I knew old Israel Porter was a part of it—and his son, Benjamin, and his grandson, Giles," Parris went on. "When you left the church this year past, I knew you were turning your back on me, but I never thought you would attack me. It was Thomas Putnam who told me anyone who was not for me was against me. He warned me that when you came back to the Salem Village church, it was to pick up the work Israel Porter had begun to take the very land out from under me. But I never wholly believed him—until now."

"Why now?" Papa said.

"You're blackening my name in the village!" Reverend Parris sputtered. "You take in heathens and raise their heathen children! You deliberately go against my teachings about cleansing our society of all evil influences!"

Josiah looked down at the top of Dorcas's head resting on his chest. Dorcas was an evil influence?

"What about your teachings on the Good Samaritan?" Joseph Hutchinson said.

"Eh?"

"You stood up there in your pulpit and told us all to fashion ourselves after the Good Samaritan and help those no one else would give the time of day to."

Reverend Parris almost squealed as he cried, "I wasn't talking about the likes of Deliverance Carrier!"

"I know," Papa said. "You were talking about yourself."

Reverend Parris said nothing. At his side, Betty stared hard at her shoes.

Josiah's father shook his head. "One thing is sure, Samuel Parris. I *am* sorry for you. Come along, Josiah."

"Where are you going?" Parris whined as they turned to go.

"To Ingersoll's Inn," Papa said. "The child should at least see her mother."

The heavy door slammed and bolted behind them. As they went down the narrow steps, Josiah heard the minister screeching from the other side. "What are you about, Betty, taking up with the likes of that Hutchinson boy?"

Josiah flinched and drew Dorcas closer to him. He hated to think of Betty being in trouble because of him. *But now that I think of it,* he told himself miserably, *everyone is in trouble because of me.*

✝ ✦ ✝

Chapter Fifteen

Only one room at Ingersoll's Inn—the room just above the front door—was without a candle in its narrow window. Still, the Ordinary didn't look inviting to Josiah as they walked up to the door. Maybe it was the grim way Papa strode across the yard that made it seem unfriendly. After all, he had said he would never come to this place again.

When they opened the door and Papa's broad frame filled the doorway, all the chatter inside stopped. Papa stepped in and rewarded everyone with a cold, searching stare. Josiah stood stiffly beside him with Dorcas clinging to his shirtfront like an infant possum.

Nathaniel Ingersoll stepped out of his kitchen looking thinner and more shriveled than ever as he stood before Josiah's wide-shouldered father. But he was master of this house, and he barked up at Joseph Hutchinson without fear.

"You've no right to come here thinkin' you'll take the Carrier woman off with you. She's an official prisoner."

"Oh, stifle your whining, Ingersoll," Papa said. "I know the laws. I've only come to talk to her."

"Why?"

"I want to assure her that her child is safe."

"She has no right—"

"She's a human being, not an animal. She has every right! Now, if you'll kindly take me to her."

Nathaniel Ingersoll looked wildly around the room for support, but everyone was too busy muttering among themselves.

"I don't know," Nathaniel finally stammered. Josiah noticed that his bald head was sparkling with sweat. "I should fetch Ezekiel Cheever."

"There is no need to call for the constable," Joseph Hutchinson said. "This is your property. I don't intend to tear down doors looking for the woman. I only ask as your neighbor that you allow me to see her."

In the corner, someone stood up. Giles Porter flashed a smile at Nathaniel Ingersoll. "I don't think you can keep the woman's lawyer from her," Giles said smoothly.

Lawyer! Josiah looked quickly at his father. Papa's eyebrows shot up.

"He's not a proper lawyer!" Nathaniel said, his bald head shaking furiously.

"I can only assume that's why he's here," said Giles. "And were I going to court, I can't think of any better man than Joseph Hutchinson to stand beside me."

For a moment, Josiah thought old Israel Porter was back, blazing his smile around the room, planting ideas in people's heads that made them think they could make everything all right—then sitting down without a scratch on himself.

Nathaniel sniffed loudly. "Lawyer, eh?" he said. But since it looked as if no one was going to stand with him barring the door, he grabbed a candlestick and led Josiah and his father to the hallway and up a narrow, creaking flight of steps. Dorcas whimpered in Josiah's arms.

"Shhh," Josiah said to her. "You're going to see your mama."

"Mama?" she cried out.

By then they had reached the second floor, where a door with a large bolt separated them from the room just above the front entrance.

"Mama?" Dorcas cried again.

There was a thump from behind the door and another cry, this one thin and raspy.

"Humph," Nathaniel said. "That's the first sound she's made since Ezekiel Cheever dragged her in here."

"Certainly," Papa said. "She hears her child. Now, if you'll kindly open the door."

Once again, Nathaniel hesitated. "I don't know. Thomas Putnam said—"

"I care little what Thomas Putnam or anyone else said, Ingersoll. This is not some hard murderer you have locked up here. I assure you she'll do you no harm."

No, Josiah thought, *but Thomas Putnam will when he finds out you've let us see her.*

Still glancing anxiously over his shoulder, Nathaniel pulled back the bolt and pushed open the heavy door.

"Dorcas?" a voice crackled from inside.

Josiah could barely hold on to the baby as she scrambled to get to her mother.

"If you'll leave us alone, then, Mr. Ingersoll," Goodman

Hutchinson said, taking the candlestick from Nathaniel.

"Leave you alone with her?" Nathaniel's voice wound up into a screech.

"Aye," said Papa tightly. "Perhaps that will give you a chance to fetch Thomas Putnam."

The innkeeper scurried off like a squirrel.

The candle gave off just enough light for Josiah to make out the form of Deliverance Carrier in the dark room. No light came in through the window, and Josiah could see that it was covered in black cloth.

But the darkness didn't seem to frighten Dorcas now. She was back with her mother and that seemed to be all that mattered.

"Thank ye for takin' care of her," she said. "I had no means to do it myself."

"We did only what the Lord would want us to do," Papa said. He leaned closer to look into her eyes. "You know you're to go to court some few days hence?"

"Nay, they told me nothin'."

"Nathaniel Putnam's accused you of trespassing on his property, and of course, none but Thomas Putnam will represent him in court. The whole family acts like poppets in his hands—they and Reverend Parris."

"I've naught to fear from the Putnams," Deliverance said. "I've done nothin' wrong, and my child's safe now."

"You've plenty to fear if you go into court alone," Papa said. "They can put you in the Salem Town jail until you can pay your way out."

Deliverance stroked Dorcas's hair with her clawlike hand and shrugged. "I ain't afraid of no jail," she said stubbornly.

"Are you afraid of what they will do with your child?" Joseph Hutchinson said.

Deliverance's eyes sprang open. "Why, you'll keep her, eh?"

"Only if the court allows it." Papa shook his head. "It's more likely they'll lock her up with you. Do you want your child to grow up in a cell not big enough to lie down in?"

Deliverance began to tremble, and in her arms Dorcas whimpered.

"I haven't come here to frighten you," Josiah's father said gently. "I've only come to offer help. If you won't take it for yourself, perhaps you'll accept it for your child. Let me find you a lawyer."

Josiah held his breath as Deliverance looked from Papa to Dorcas and back again. He had never seen the inside of the Salem Town jail, but he had heard stories. The cells were cold and darker than this room, and there was space only to stand up or crouch like a mole. The thought of it made him shudder.

"I couldn't pay no lawyer," Deliverance said finally.

"I will pay, Goody Carrier," Papa said softly.

Shifting Dorcas to hold her with one arm, Deliverance waved her free hand in the air. "I can come to yer door and crawl for yer leftover stew, because I hope in my heart I can someday pay ye back. But that kind of money, it's sure I'll never have means to get it back to ye."

Her voice broke, and she turned her face away.

"You shall repay me," Papa said. "There's work aplenty on our farm, enough to make you clear of debt before the child can learn to talk. You trusted me to take care of your child, so why not trust that I am as good as my word?"

"Ach!" Deliverance slapped her hand against the tears on her cheek, and her shiny eyes darted toward Josiah. "It weren't ye I trusted," she said. "It were him."

Josiah looked at the toes of his boots. *Why would you trust me*, he thought bleakly. *I'm naught but a foolish boy who thought himself a man.*

"All right, then," his father said. "Trust in me because I'm the boy's father."

Josiah stole a look at Deliverance. She said nothing as her faded eyes went from Josiah to his father and back again, as if to find some answer in their faces.

"Does that mean yes, Goody Carrier?" Papa said. She only nodded. "Good, then. At first light I'll be off to Salem Town. I've friends there who will know the best man to be at your side in court. See you rest now. You've a fight ahead of you."

The woman's shoulders sagged, and Josiah thought he'd never seen anyone who looked less ready for a fight. She hugged Dorcas close to her and pulled one of her tiny hands up to her lips. It was still balled up into a tight little fist, and as Deliverance uncurled the fingers to kiss them, something floated to the floor. Papa bent over to pick it up, his face puzzled.

"The child was clutching a rag?" he said.

Josiah recognized it right away. It was the piece of Deliverance's skirt he had seen in the lean-to when he and Dorcas had first arrived there. Dorcas must have kept it clutched in her little fist all this time. *It must have made her feel closer to her mother*, he thought. *It must have made her feel safer*.

"What? Have ye something in yer other hand, too?"

Deliverance was saying. She pried open the fingers of Dorcas's other fist. There in her pink palm was Josiah's whistle pouch. Deliverance blinked at it.

"Where did ye find such a thing?" she said, and then she shook her head. "Yer a queer sort of child," she said. "Keep it, then. Ye haven't much else."

Josiah gave a sigh of relief as Dorcas curled her fingers back around the pouch. Nobody had figured out that it belonged to him. There would be no end to the teasing. But there his thoughts stumbled. *That must have made her feel safer, too. At least I did something right.*

As his father nodded to him, Josiah quickly stepped forward to take Dorcas from her mother. It would still be better if nobody else knew that. He was feeling unmanly enough as it was.

"Get ye to the sawmill at dawn, Josiah," his father said, bolting the door behind him. Then as they made their way down the dark staircase, he contiued, "I must go to Salem Town and see Phillip English, though I fear we'll have to go all the way to Boston to find a lawyer."

"Go wherever you like, Joseph Hutchinson," said a voice at the bottom of the steps. "But the woman built herself a house on Putnam land, and that's plain fact. If she wants a place to live, Salem Town will give her a cell."

Papa stopped so short that Josiah nearly plowed into him with Dorcas in his arms. He peered around his father to see Thomas Putnam's big face reddening in the light of the candle he held. Dorcas whimpered and dug her face into Josiah's shirt.

"Give us a light here, Putnam," Goodman Hutchinson said. "I want to discuss this matter face to face."

Thomas held up the flickering flame, and Josiah's father moved quickly toward him with Josiah and Dorcas at his heels.

"What is there to discuss, Hutchinson?" Thomas Putnam said, setting the candle on a small table by the stairway. "My son and nephews found the woman in some crude shack."

"I know the story, Thomas," Papa said.

"You know *her* side of it. But you'd best know all the facts if you're to represent her before the magistrates."

"Ach! I've no intention of doing anything of the kind! Unlike you, I don't fool myself into thinking I am an official of the court."

Thomas's eyes bulged. "I shall state the facts to the magistrates. I don't need to be a lawyer to know when trespassing— nay, stealing—has taken place on my family's property. . . ."

"*Stealing!*" Joseph Hutchinson cried. "What has she stolen?"

"My brother's land! The woman intended to take up permanent residence as if it belonged to her!"

"Permanent residence? On that pitiful piece of ground? Thomas, she's a poor widow who was starving and without a bed because of selfish, stiff-necked people like you—people who wouldn't give her a corner of your miserable barn to sleep in. She had naught to do but fashion some shelter for herself on a lifeless patch of land she was certain nobody else would have!"

"We Putnams are tired of your insults to our property!" Thomas stammered.

"And we Hutchinsons are tired of your unchristian ways. They make it impossible for God-fearing people to live in peace in this village. I will see you in court, Putnam. And God willing, I'll see you shamed for the foolish, covetous man you are."

Thomas's eyes blazed. "Then you *will* act as her lawyer?"

"Aye, and as God's representative."

"God's!"

"Someone in this village has to speak for Him."

With that, Joseph Hutchinson strode from the dark hallway. For the first time that evening, Thomas's wet, bulbous eyes lit on Josiah. He put a rough hand on Josiah's shoulder to stop him, and Dorcas screamed and burrowed herself into his chest.

"What have you to do with this, boy?" Thomas Putnam said. "If there's trouble, it's sure you're in the middle of it!"

Papa moved back toward Thomas Putnam, and he folded his own big fingers around the man's arm. His eyes were tight under his furious brows. "Let go of my son, Putnam."

Thomas stared at the hand that squeezed angry folds into his sleeve. Josiah saw him gulp as he released his hold on his shoulder. Josiah stepped quickly to his father's side.

There was a long silence as Papa's fiery eyes lit into Thomas Putnam's. When Papa finally spoke, every word came out like the blade of a knife slashing the air. "If I find that you—or any of the rest of your savage brood—ever touch one of my children, may God have mercy on your soul."

Thomas's eyes swam. "Are you threatening me, Hutchinson?" he said, his voice shaking.

"Nay, that is no threat," Joseph Hutchinson answered. "'Tis a promise."

They left Ingersoll's Ordinary without another word, and

Josiah had to run with Dorcas bouncing against him to keep up with his father's long, livid strides. But they had barely reached the road when the inn door flew open behind them.

"Joseph!" Giles Porter called out. "Wait!"

Papa seemed reluctant to stop even for him, but he turned around and sighed. Josiah watched from his elbow.

"So you are going to act as the woman's lawyer, eh?" Giles said when he caught up to them. His handsome Porter eyes were twinkling.

"Aye," Papa said wearily.

"I'm glad I put the idea into your head!"

"It wasn't you who put it there, Giles. 'Twas God."

For a moment, Giles's smile seemed to be painted on his face. "God?" he said.

"Aye. Am I the only man left in this village who goes to the Lord for guidance?"

"Of course not, Joseph! We pray every day that God will work some miracle in this society and we will have peace at last."

"Do you?"

Even Josiah was startled by the venom in his father's voice. Giles took a step back.

"Aye, we do," Giles said. "What is it that bothers you, Joseph?"

"We've planned ways of restoring peace to the church, but I told you, and your uncle Benjamin, and even your grandfather before he went to his grave, that I would not be a part of any underhanded plot."

The dazzling Porter smile came back to Giles's face. "We plan to put the church back into the hands of good Christians, where it belongs. You make it sound as if we have some conspiracy afoot!" He gave a practiced chuckle. "'Tis no 'plot,' Joseph!"

"Then what was Reverend Parris talking about tonight? He spoke of a scheme to run him out of the church—the work Israel Porter began."

Giles laughed softly. "You know Parris is afraid of his own shadow. He's built up this grand scheme in his own mind, and it's sure Thomas Putnam and his brothers planted the seed for it."

There was a stiff moment as Joseph Hutchinson stared hard at Giles Porter. "I pray you're telling me the truth," he said finally in a hard voice. "I did not agree to do anything underhanded or deceitful, and it's sure I never knew anyone wanted to run Mr. Parris out of his position."

"Joseph, don't you want the church out of the hands of the Putnams?"

"Aye! I want it out of the hands of any man and back into the hands of God!"

"Do you not believe that's what we are trying to do?" Giles said. His voice was coaxing. Josiah could feel his father hardening beside him.

"I don't know what to believe. I go to God, and I do as He counsels."

"And He counsels you to go to court with the beggar woman and fight Thomas Putnam and his brothers!" Giles cried. "Their evil influence is everywhere, and we must stop them however we can. God has made you part of that. Don't you see?"

Papa shook his head. "No, I don't see. But I pray that soon I shall. I pray it with all my heart." His eyes zeroed in on

Giles for a moment before he said, "Just be certain you're telling me the truth." Then he turned and crunched his heels across the stones toward home. Josiah stole one last backward glance as he followed.

There was no dazzling smile on Giles Porter's face.

✞ ✦ ✞

Chapter Sixteen

orcas was already sleeping when Josiah tumbled her into Hope's big bed. Hope sat up like a shot and looked at him with wild eyes. Josiah could tell she had been having a bad dream again.

"Is she safe?" she said.

"Aye," Josiah said. "Look at her."

"And what of Deliverance Carrier? Did the Putnams hurt her?"

"No! And Papa won't let them either."

Hope shook her head and fell fitfully back onto her pillows. "Papa can't stop them. No one can stop them."

Her eyes closed, and she fell back into her troubled dreams, but Josiah shook his head. He thought of Papa's words: *If I find that you—or any of the rest of your savage brood—ever touch one of my children, may God have mercy on your soul.* It was in his hands now—a *real* man's hands.

Slowly, Josiah went to the window and sat forlornly on the chest. He knew he should feel safe now that his father was in charge, but mostly he just felt disappointed—in himself. The more he had tried to do it on his own, the worse things had gotten.

Papa is a real man, Josiah thought. *He shoulders it all and with no one's help now that old Israel is gone.*

But suddenly it was as if a toe had been stuck into Josiah's thoughts and set them all to stumbling over themselves. What was it his father had said tonight? *Am I the only man left in this village who goes to the Lord for guidance?*

Was that the secret to Papa's strength and wisdom—that he didn't do it alone? That he went to God?

But what about when God was so far away? Where had He been when Hope was attacked by the Putnams? Or when they discovered Josiah at Deliverance's lean-to? Or when the bear found Josiah and Deliverance in the woods?

Josiah's sleepy eyes wandered over the room. When they caught on Hope's bed, they sprang open.

Evidently, God had been right there. Why else was Hope safely asleep in her bed now or he sitting right here at the window? Who else had put the idea into Hope's head that let her escape from the Putnams? Who else let him think of giving the bear the food in the bag?

"'Twas God," Papa had said to Giles Porter.

Josiah wearily rested his head on the chest. That was fine, he thought. But why did God always have to be so hard to find?

He'd have to look for Him again. Maybe tomorrow.

It wasn't until dinner was over and his work done the next day that Josiah had a chance to search. And when Mama

handed him a bucket and told him to go out and see if any
berries had yet shown themselves in the woods, he wasn't
sure where to go. He let his footsteps wander until he found
himself on a crooked piece of land just below Hathorne's Hill.
It was the Blessing Place.

Josiah pushed at the ground with his toe and uncovered a
blackened spot from last winter's fire. He turned the bucket
over and sat down on it, just as he'd once sat inside the shack
and prayed for God's help. But now the words to pray just
wouldn't come. They all seemed to be crowded out by shouts
of *You can't do it, Josiah. You're not a man. You can't do anything alone.*

"Then don't let me be alone!" Josiah finally cried out
loud. "Please, please, God, put the ideas in my head!"

Tears crept up behind his eyelids, and Josiah smeared at
them with the backs of his hands. *I never used to cry so
much*, he thought. *Just last winter I was the leader of the
Merry Band. We sat right here and made our plans, and I
never cried then.*

Josiah leaned over and absently pulled up a blade of grass
that was bravely sprouting at the edge of the charred ground.
The last time the Merry Band had met here after the shack
had burned down, they had promised to come here again—
together—to think of only good deeds to do to help their
parents. Right now, his father was doing the good deeds.
What was left for the Merry Band to do? Every time they tried
to help, they only made their war with the Putnams worse.

Josiah stood up with a jerk that set the bucket tumbling.
That was it. Why not do the best deed of all and stop the war
once and for all? He wasn't sure how, but that was what the

Merry Band did best. They put their heads together, and they planned.

Josiah snatched up the bucket and took off at a run toward Wolf Pits Meadow. Hope would be too afraid to come, and Rachel and Ezekiel were out of the question. But there were always Sarah and William. Three could think of something.

And there was also another friend Josiah knew he could trust.

It was too spectacular a sunset evening for anyone to be stuck inside, but Josiah took a chance and, hiding in the underbrush, tossed a handful of pebbles up at Betty Parris's window. He ducked and held his breath to watch through the twigs, barely daring to hope.

Her wispy blonde head appeared and she poked it out to look below.

"Psst!" Josiah hissed to her.

Within minutes, she was scurrying across the parsonage yard, glancing nervously over her shoulder as she ran.

She hasn't done this kind of thing before, Josiah thought with a grin. *Anyone passing by would know she was on a secret mission.*

But her eyes were shining when she safely reached the bushes and squeezed in beside Josiah.

"How is the little angel?" she said.

"Fine," Josiah said, waving his hand impatiently. "Do you want to be part of a plan?"

Betty's eyes widened until Josiah thought they would nearly take over her thin, little face. "What kind of plan?" she said.

"A plan to help stop all this fighting in the village."

The big eyes narrowed until Josiah almost laughed. She was trying hard to look like Abigail and failing miserably.

"Will it hurt my papa?" she said.

"No! It will probably even help him. I promise."

She searched his eyes for so long that Josiah glanced anxiously at the sky. He would never understand girls. Why could they never just decide?

"All right, then," Betty said finally. She rubbed her white hands together. "What would you have me do?"

"You know those messages you've sent me, on paper?"

"Aye."

"Can you get one to William and Sarah Proctor?"

"I think I can. What should I say?"

"That there's to be a meeting of the Merry Band," he said.

Josiah's feet nearly flew as he ran down the road toward the Hutchinson farm. He knew Betty was still there in the bushes watching him, with the information tucked safely in her head.

Time dragged its feet until the next day at sunset. At least three times that day, Josiah almost told Hope about the meeting and begged her to come. But every time, he caught the wild, frightened look in her eyes, and he knew she'd never do it—that she'd probably plead with him not to go either.

The only time her eyes seemed calm was when she was playing with Dorcas in a patch of sun outside the kitchen. Maybe the best thing was for her to stay here and take care of Deliverance Carrier's little girl, he decided. That was how she could help.

With Papa still gone to Salem Town, the way was clear for Josiah to dash toward the Blessing Place again at sunset. But his stomach still fluttered as he walked up the road toward Hathorne's Hill, trying not to look as if he were going anywhere special.

I'm nearly as bad as Betty Parris, he thought. And then he smiled. As much of a rabbit as she might be about such affairs, she got the job done. He'd found a tiny piece of parchment tucked into the woodpile after dinner. "Deliverd yer messidg," it had said.

Now if Sarah and William would only answer it.

But Josiah's thoughts were interrupted by the sound of hoofbeats around the bend. He started to dash for the woods when he heard a voice like fresh air calling out to him.

"Hello there, Captain!" Joseph Putnam shouted.

Josiah went toward him as Joseph reined in his horse and smiled down at him.

"I'll be glad when school begins again," he said to Josiah. "These times between our chats are too long, eh?"

Josiah nodded nervously.

"We shall talk soon, then, eh?" Joseph said. "Perhaps later tonight. I'm headed for your house now. Is your father back from Salem Town yet?"

"No, sir," Josiah said. "We don't expect him until after dark."

"Of course. I'm just a bit anxious. I've given it some thought and some prayer, Captain, and I've decided that your father should not have to handle this Deliverance Carrier situation alone. It's a sign of what is happening to all of us in this village, and I think all of us who want peace need to stand together."

Joseph's handsome face was flushed, but it quickly broke into a grin. "I get a bit passionate about these things sometimes, Captain. Perhaps your mother has some apple cider and pie to calm me down while I wait, eh?" His eyes twinkled. "That is, if you didn't polish it all off at supper. Do you know you've grown several hands higher since winter, Captain? You're becoming a fine young man."

A pang went through Josiah. *If only that were true.*

"So where are you off to, then?" Joseph said.

Josiah shifted anxiously and looked in the direction of Hathorne's Hill. He hated to lie to Joseph, but . . .

Why did he have to lie? What was wrong with the Merry Band meeting to talk? Why couldn't this man, who thought Josiah, too, was a man, know what he was about? After all, they were all working for the same thing.

When Josiah looked up at him, Joseph Putnam was watching him patiently.

"I've called a meeting of . . . my friends," Josiah said. "We're going up to the spot where our hideout burned last winter."

Joseph cocked a curious eyebrow. "An odd place to play, so close to the Putnams."

"We aren't going to play exactly," Josiah said slowly. Would Joseph think his plan silly? What if he told him they shouldn't even try it?

"Perhaps it's not my business to ask—"

"We want to stop our war with the Putnam boys!" Josiah blurted out. "We want to find some peaceful way. It's gone too far. People are getting hurt . . . " Josiah's voice trailed off.

"You're a good man, Josiah Hutchinson," Joseph said. "Just see you be careful. Don't try to do it alone. There are always friends to help you." He started to tip his hat, and then stopped to add, "Will Ezekiel be joining you, then?"

"No, sir."

"Still haven't talked out your differences, you two?"

Josiah just shook his head.

"That's your only real problem, then, Captain."

Josiah looked at him sharply. "Until you forgive," Joseph said, "you're always alone in your heart." This time he did tip his hat, and then he rode away.

Josiah sat at the Blessing Place until the sun threatened to dip behind Hathorne's Hill. He was ready to give up and go home when two silhouettes appeared.

"You would pick a spot on top of Putnam land!" William said breathlessly when they reached him. "We had to go practically 'round the world to get here without one of them snatching us up!"

Sarah looked around. "Where's Hope?" she said.

"She . . . she didn't come."

Sarah's shoulders sagged. "Oh. I wanted to see her. We haven't talked since . . ." She squinted to remember.

"Since the day I played the bear?" Josiah said.

Sarah nodded thoughtfully. "Aye, it was then. Even at Israel Porter's funeral, she seemed so far away." Her lower lip started to tremble. "I thought perhaps she was mad at me, and now I know it for sure!"

William groaned. "Don't start crying again, Sarah. I hate it when you do that."

"She wasn't mad at you," Josiah said quickly. He didn't much relish the thought of Sarah bursting into tears either. "She won't talk to anyone anymore. She's too frightened."

"Frightened?" William snorted. "Hope? She isn't afraid of anything!"

"She is now, and it's the Putnams that did it to her. That's why I asked you to come here. We have to do something to stop this war. It's gone too far."

All the color had by now drained from Sarah's face, and she clawed at Josiah's sleeve. "What happened to her, Josiah?"

"I don't know all of it. But I'll tell you what I've figured out."

The three of them sat in a tight knot as Josiah began.

"That day, when the Putnams surprised us, you two ran home. I hid in the trap and Hope took off toward Hathorne's Great Swamp with the Putnams after her. I thought surely she'd lose them and then turn back for our house." Josiah swallowed hard. "I should have gone after them, but she's always wanted to do everything herself. Anyway, I got home late and she still wasn't there. When she did come home, there was this look all over her face."

"What kind of look?" William asked.

"Like she'd seen the devil himself. But every time I asked her, she would just explode like a musket, and then she'd beg me to be careful every time I went out the door. She kept telling me the Putnams were more dangerous than any of us ever imagined. Every day it seemed like she was more and more scared. She wasn't even acting like Hope anymore. The day we discovered the widow's cabin had been chopped down, she was screamin' and cryin'. I thought she'd sure go mad right there in the woods. She's having bad dreams. It's as if she's just . . . given up hope."

Josiah stopped and blinked his eyes hard. It felt good to

have it all pouring out of him at last, but tears were threatening to come with it. He couldn't cry now.

"What do you think they did to her?" Sarah whispered as if she were afraid to say the words.

"I think it had something to do with Jonathon Putnam's knife," Josiah said.

Sarah gasped, and even William caught his breath.

"He has a knife now," Josiah went on. "I saw it the day Papa and I were beating the bounds, and when I mentioned it to Hope, she . . . well, she looked as if someone were holding the blade to her throat right then and there."

"You don't really think they did that, do you?" Sarah said.

"It's almost certain they did," Josiah said. "Another day when they chased me off Thomas Putnam's property, Eleazer almost let it slip out."

"Aye, he's a stupid one," William said.

"I don't care how stupid they are," Sarah cried. "Hope is right. They're dangerous!" She turned her eyes, swimming in tears, on Josiah. "We can't do anything to stop people with weapons, Josiah."

"But the knife is gone now!" Josiah said. "When they tied me up, the same night they found Deliverance Carrier on Nathaniel Putnam's land, Eleazer said, 'If we had our knife.' Don't you see? Now is the perfect time to put a stop to this war. They don't have their weapon, and maybe we can convince Hope to tell them that if they don't stop causing trouble, she will tell everyone in the village what they did to her, whatever it was."

"And I think whatever it was is much worse than we can imagine," Sarah said. "I know Hope. It would take something horrible to frighten her like this."

"Then you'll help?" Josiah said.

She looked at him out of a face the color of snow, and Josiah's heart sank. This rabbit of a girl was never going to go after the Putnams with her little brother and his friend, who had nothing to fight with but big ideas.

But Sarah tilted her chin up and blinked back the tears. "She would do the same for me," she said. "And she would have done it long before this."

"So what do you want to do?" William said.

Josiah frowned. "I know I want to get the Putnams where we can talk to them, without worrying about them attacking us. We have to be in control just for a few minutes. But I don't have even one idea how to do that."

There was a disappointed silence.

"I do," William said suddenly.

Sarah stared. "You do?"

"Aye. You remember the last time the Merry Band was together? The day of the bear trap?"

They nodded.

"Who do you think laid that trap for you, Mr. Bear?"

"I thought it was just some . . . " Josiah stopped as a slow grin spread over his face. "You, William? 'Twas you?"

"Not me alone," William said.

Josiah followed his gaze to Sarah, who was starting to smile.

"It can't be!" Josiah cried.

"Do you think me some helpless ninny like Abigail Williams?" Sarah said. "We Proctors know how to use a shovel."

"You're saying we should build a trap for the Putnams and catch them in it long enough to offer them our deal?" Josiah said.

William looked down at his boot tops and shrugged. "Perhaps it isn't such a good idea."

"Nay, it's perfect!" Josiah cried. He glanced up at the sky. "It's nearly dark. Let's get started."

The sun had disappeared behind Hathorne's Hill by the time all the pieces of the plan were in place, and Josiah felt the old glow of excitement when it was done. Only twice as they bent their heads together in thought did he feel a stab of anything doubtful.

Once was when he suggested that Betty Parris be involved. "She's the enemy," Sarah said stubbornly.

"But isn't that what we're trying to do?" Josiah protested. "Make it so there are no more enemies?"

Both William and Sarah grew quiet, and Josiah took that as a yes.

The other stab came when William rocked back on his knees and said, "This would be so much easier had we Rachel and Ezekiel with us."

Sarah's eyes darted over to Josiah, and then she looked down at her hands.

"I could ask Ezekiel," William said. "You wouldn't even have to talk to him, Josiah."

"No!" Josiah said. "If he's to join us, I won't be a part of it."

"You'll let in a Parris but not a Porter?" Sarah said timidly.

"Not a Porter who's proven himself to be a traitor," Josiah said.

There was silence, and they went on with the plan. As the sun blinked out over Salem Village, the three returned to their houses. Nothing more was said about Ezekiel and Rachel Porter.

✞ ✦ ✞

Chapter Seventeen

hen Josiah got home, the wagon was pulled up to the barn and the oxen were waiting and snorting for their supper. Josiah hurried to feed them and put the wagon away so he would have time to talk more with Joseph Putnam. But Papa and Joseph were already standing on the front steps, saying their good-byes, when Josiah sailed around the corner.

"Two days—that's soon," Joseph Putnam was saying. "It gives us little time to prepare ourselves."

"I only thank the Lord you're willing to help me. This is the work of two men, I think."

"And more would be better. Do you not think Benjamin Porter might assist? Or young Giles?"

Papa shook his head. "John Proctor will come to give us support, though he's not one to talk in public. But the Porters—" He stopped as his eye caught on Josiah.

"Josiah, I've news of your Deliverance Carrier," he said. "She's to be allowed to stay in Ingersoll's Inn since we go to court only two days from now."

Joseph Putnam put his hand on Josiah's shoulder. "That was decided only after your father agreed to pay for her food and board, mind you. Joseph, I beg you to reconsider—let me pay for half."

Goodman Hutchinson waved his hand. "Ach. It matters not who pays, so long as the poor woman doesn't have to rot in their stinking jail. You're doing enough, Joseph, just standing by me in this. I could not do it alone."

Josiah stared at his father. *I could not do it alone.* Those were words he was hearing a lot lately in his own head. He never thought he would hear them come from Papa's mouth.

But as the two men shook hands and Joseph Putnam rode off, other, more important words were spinning in Josiah's mind. *Two days hence.* If Papa and Sarah and William's father were going to be gone then, and the Putnams as well, that was the perfect time to execute their plan.

But two days. There was so much to be done.

Josiah and William started the next evening at sunset, when, with shovels in hand, they slid in and out of the shadows toward the base of Thorndike Hill, just on the safe side of Nathaniel Putnam's property line, and began to dig.

"Two nights will never be enough time to dig a pit deep enough for those tall Putnam boys," William moaned at the end of the first night, as he examined the blisters on his hands.

"It wouldn't be enough time for one of us alone," Josiah told him. "But for both of us working together—" Josiah snapped his fingers.

"I don't know," William mumbled. He didn't add what Josiah knew he was thinking. *It would be so much easier if we had Ezekiel, too.*

The next night, as Josiah sat on the chest by the window looking down on Salem Village he decided that building the trap had been the easy part. There were two hard things still left to be done. Luring the Putnam boys out to the right place at the right time was one. After his visit to the bushes at the parsonage this afternoon, that was up to Betty Parris now.

The other was getting Hope to go with them and convincing her to talk to the Putnams while they were safely tucked in the trap. That was up to Sarah.

This plan would never have worked if he had tried to do it all on his own. Josiah knew that now. For a second, he closed his eyes and said out loud, "Thank you."

"Who's there?" Hope cried out in her sleep.

"'Tis only me," Josiah called softly to her. "Me and God."

The day of the plan dawned soft and shiny, and Josiah took that as a sign that all was going to go well. His spirits were so high that he volunteered to load Papa's wagon with the things he would need in Salem Town. Awhile later, he stood at the corner of the yard with Dorcas on his shoulders waving good-bye.

"They're going to help your mama," he said to her. "They'll bring her back, I know it."

"Mama?" Dorcas said.

"You haven't forgotten her, have you?" Josiah said.

But she curled her fingers into his hair and cried, "'Siah! Horsie!"

Then nothing would do but for him to gallop across the yard with her bouncing and squealing on his shoulders as she yanked his curls. It almost didn't matter if anyone saw him, because soon, very soon, this was all going to be over.

But in midafternoon, when Josiah was chopping wood for the supper fire, the door opened and Mama stepped out, wearing her bonnet and no apron. She was carrying a large basket covered with a napkin.

"Josiah," she said, "I've told Hope I want the two of you to watch over Dorcas for me and tend to the supper. I must make the rounds of the houses of our friends and gather food to replace what Nathaniel Ingersoll's fed Deliverance at the inn."

"Now?" Josiah said. His heart was rapidly picking up speed inside his chest.

"Aye," his mother answered. She looked at him curiously. "Is there some reason why I shouldn't?"

"No, ma'am!" Josiah said quickly. "But when will you come home?"

"Well after dark, I think," she said. She smiled her shy smile. "Don't worry yourself, Josiah. Hope will be sure you're fed. You've the appetite of a Massachusetts brown bear of late."

But who's to watch over Dorcas while we go to meet the Putnams? he wanted to cry after her as she went down the road. They couldn't possibly take her along. He'd already put her in enough danger. Only thanks to Betty Parris had they gotten her away from the Putnams the last time.

Betty Parris. Of course.

Josiah ran to the house with an armload of wood, dumped it noisily on the hearth, and ran for the door again.

"Where do you think you're off to, Josiah Hutchinson?" Hope said.

"I've one more thing to take care of—an errand."

"I know of no errand," Hope said.

Josiah ignored her and pulled open the door.

"Josiah, please, don't leave me here alone."

Josiah turned and stared at her. Her face had gone the color of ashes, and she wrung her apron with her hands. "Please," she whispered again.

"I shan't be gone long, I promise," he said. "Bolt the door behind me and you'll be safe."

As he tore off across the yard, he heard the seldom-used bolt slide into place. And he heard his sister crying against the door. *It will all be over tonight, Hope,* he thought.

After throwing pebbles at Betty's window, Josiah hid in the underbrush until he thought he'd grow old waiting. When he heard rustling behind him, it wasn't a pale face that peeked between the twigs, but a dark one.

"Betty bid me come," Tituba said. "She cannot. She say— message." She pointed from Josiah to herself. "She say please—want to help." And then she leaned forward and put a warm hand on Josiah's arm. The look in her black eyes was warm and glossy, just like Betty's. Perhaps that was where Betty had learned to be so kind . . . and so brave.

"Please ask her to be here as soon as the sun goes down if she can," Josiah said. "I need her to take care of Dorcas for just a little while."

"Ah, the angel! We will do."

Tituba nodded her head until Josiah was sure it would bob right off her shoulders. When he looked back as he ran toward home, she was hurrying toward the parsonage, still bobbing.

By the time he returned to the kitchen, Sarah and William were there, and Hope's eyes were snapping again.

"William says you two have some kind of nighttime game planned, Josiah," she said, arms folded across her chest. "But you are not leaving me with—"

"We'll take Dorcas with us," Josiah said. He could feel William and Sarah looking at him in horror, but he snatched up Dorcas from her chair and tumbled her over his shoulders. She clutched at her bread and giggled.

"You are not going to take that baby out into the—"

"She'll be perfectly safe. I promise," Josiah said with more confidence than he felt. "And if we're not back in half an hour, you can come look for me and drag me home by the ear!"

"Josiah, no!"

"Come on, William," Josiah said, and together they fled from the kitchen and out the front door. In spite of Dorcas's chirping in his ear, he could still hear Hope pleading with him as they took off across the yard.

"Have you gone mad?" William hissed to him as they scooped up the rope and bag of long grass they had hidden by a bush and ran from the yard. He jabbed a finger toward Dorcas. "How can we do this with *her* along?"

"She isn't coming along," Josiah said, heading for the underbrush at the edge of the parsonage yard. "And she has just given Sarah a reason to lure Hope out of the house."

There was no more time for questions, for they had reached the thicket, and two stick-like white arms stuck out between the twigs.

"When will you come back for her?" Betty said.

"One hour," Josiah said. "Can you keep her that long?"

"Aye. 'Tis only Tituba and me. Just throw a stone at the kitchen window."

"You *have* gone mad," William whispered as they hurried away. "You're leaving her with Betty *Parris?*"

"She only looks like Betty Parris," Josiah said. "It's really an angel."

William was still muttering about it when they reached the base of Thorndike Hill.

"Shut it, would you please, William?" Josiah said. "Let's just check the trap, eh?"

William's face brightened immediately as he examined his handiwork. A perfect network of crossed branches and a thick carpet of leaves concealed a pit big enough for four Putnams to fall into and deep enough to keep them there . . . for a while.

"I'd have fallen into it myself if I hadn't known exactly where it was," William said, chest puffed out. "The Putnams are ours, Josiah."

"Aye."

"That is, if they come at all." William's almost-white eyebrows puckered. "Do you think they'll be curious enough to—?"

But before he could finish, Josiah clapped his hand over William's mouth and pointed. Whipping down the road below them toward Nathaniel Putnam's house were Richard, Silas, and Eleazer. Richard was waving a piece of parchment over his head.

"They got their messages with the maps on them. They're going to get Jonathon," Josiah told William almost soundlessly. "They'll be here."

That was another piece that had fallen into place. Josiah peered anxiously into the gathering darkness. Now if Sarah would only get here with Hope.

There was a crackling sound above them, and Josiah looked up hopefully. But the hill was silent.

"There, yonder. By the brook," William whispered, pointing below. "I see Sarah's cap."

As Sarah's cap wobbled toward them, another appeared, a head below it.

Sarah was nearly carrying Hope up the hill as she clung to Sarah's arm with both hands. Her face was smashed against Sarah's sleeve, as if whatever she couldn't see wouldn't be there. *Only a little while longer*, Josiah thought fiercely. *Please, please, God, don't let us be alone in this*.

Almost at the same moment, Sarah reached them with Hope still attached to her, and William spotted the Putnam boys creeping from the edge of Nathaniel Putnam's property and starting up the hill. He pointed feverishly toward the hiding place he and Josiah had picked out last night, and Josiah shoved Sarah toward it. Hope pulled her face away from Sarah's sleeve and opened her mouth.

"No, be silent, Hope!" Sarah whispered, too quietly for Hope to hear.

Josiah grabbed both sides of his sister's face and turned it toward him. He shook his head hard. The eyes that looked back into his were blinking with fear, but Hope closed her mouth and followed William into the thicket of bushes.

"The map says here!" they heard Eleazer belt out from just below them. "Your knife should be buried just up the slope."

"I tell you, this is some kind of trick!" Silas said.

"What if it is?" Jonathon answered him with a snort. "Anyone can plan a trick against the Putnams, but how many can outwit them, eh?"

There was a chorus of agreeing grunts and murmurs.

"If it be a trick, we shall have revenge," Jonathon went on. "And if this be the work of some secret friend, I shall have my knife back. I see no threat to the Putnams here."

"Still, I say we tread carefully," Silas muttered.

"Good, then, ninny," Eleazer said. "*You* tread carefully."

They should nearly be at the trap by now. Josiah dared a peek past a leaf and sucked in his breath. Silas was walking ahead of the other three, carefully examining the ground through the darkness. Two more steps and he might see a slight unevenness in the dirt, or—

"No!" came a piercing cry from beside him. Hope gasped for air and screamed again. "No! Please don't hurt me!"

Four surprised faces came up before them. Four angry pairs of legs started across the clearing toward them.

And four bodies fell, screaming, into a dark pit.

✢ ⋅✢⋅ ✢

Chapter Eighteen

"Now!" Josiah whispered to William and Sarah. They grabbed the bushes they were hiding behind and crashed the branches against each other. Hope sank to her knees and sobbed silently.

"RAAAHHHHHHHR!" Josiah roared.

The pit grew stone-still.

"RAAAHHHHHHHR!" Josiah roared again and nodded for William and Sarah to keep rustling.

"It's a bear!" Eleazer cried. His voice teetered on the edge of tears and was answered by a loud smack.

Josiah grinned at William through the darkness.

"RAAAHHHHHHHHR!" he roared one last time. William and Sarah stopped crashing, and Josiah panted loudly.

"He smells us!" Eleazer squeaked out. The slap that followed was fainter this time, and Josiah knew he had them going. It was time.

He crouched down and put his mouth close to Hope's ear.

"It's your turn now, Hope," he whispered. "Tell them that

172

now they know how it feels to be frightened to death by some stupid trick. Now the war can be over, because we're even. Tell them they have to keep the peace—or you'll tell what they did to you."

For days, Josiah had been waiting for the look that would appear on Hope's face when she realized she was finally safe. Her eyes would take on their old sparkle again, and she would stomp over to the edge of the pit with her hands on her hips and have her moment of glory.

But there was only sheer terror in the eyes that searched for his in the night.

"Please, Josiah," she said in a broken voice. "Let us just get away!"

"But it can be all done with, once and for all. Don't you see?"

She shook her head and sobbed until Josiah thought she would choke. This was not the way it was supposed to be.

"Do you think he's gone?" they heard Richard say from the pit.

William and Sarah quickly rattled the bushes and shot questioning looks toward Josiah.

Slowly, he got up and went to the edge of the pit. Four terrified faces jerked toward him, and four pairs of eyes melted in relief.

"There's no bear up here," Josiah said.

"It's the village idiot!" Jonathon said. The jeering edge snapped back into his voice.

"I told you it was a trick," Silas said.

"It was a trick," Josiah said. "But not the kind you Putnams play."

Jonathon's lip curled. "'Tis a lame trick."

"No, it's a trick to stop this stupid war—once and for all."

"How, idiot?"

"Now that you know how it feels to be frightened half out of your minds, the score is even."

Jonathon threw his big, bulbous head back and spewed out a laugh. "Who was frightened half out of their minds?"

"You were, Jonathon Putnam, and your cousins, too. We heard you."

"So how does this fear you've imagined stop the war?" Jonathon said.

Josiah bit his lip. At this point, he wasn't sure. Without Hope speaking up, there really wasn't much they could do. The Merry Band needed her; they couldn't do it alone. He could almost hear Joseph Putnam telling him—

Of course! That was it.

"Because we've done our part," Josiah said slowly. "Now you have only to do yours: Promise to stop your side of the war, and we'll let you out of there."

"Your part?" Jonathon shot back at him. "What is your part?"

"We've forgiven you," Josiah said.

There was only a second or two of silence before the pit exploded with Putnam snorts and guffaws. Even William and Sarah were gaping at Josiah in disbelief. Hope had stopped crying, but she only stared at her brother with a blank face. Josiah wasn't sure he had ever felt more like an idiot—yet what else was there to do?

And then, from the pit, a voice broke through the raucous laughter.

"All right! I'll agree to that!"

"Agree to what, Silas?" Jonathon said, still chortling through his nose.

"To stop the war. Let me out, and I'll promise."

Josiah went down on hands and knees and peered into the pit at Silas. The face lifted up to his was sober and sorry.

Jonathon grabbed Silas by the back of the neck.

"Now who's the village idiot?" he cried.

"Let go of me, Jonathon! I'll not have you bullying me more, and I won't be a part of your tricks and your cruelty!"

"You're *not* part of them. You weren't even there when we took the Hutchinson girl, and I'm glad of it. You're naught but a ninny!"

"I was part of it because I'm a Putnam. Perhaps I can't change my name, but I can change my ways." Silas looked up at Josiah again. "Though I had no part in what they did to your sister, I apologize for all of them," he said. "Will you let me out?"

But before Josiah could motion for William to hand him the rope, Jonathon yanked his cousin back by the hair and thrust him to the floor of the pit. Within seconds, it was hard to tell whose legs and arms were whose as Richard and Eleazer dove on top of him with Jonathon shouting instructions.

"Hit him! Beat him to a bloody pulp!"

"Stop! Stop it now!" someone screamed.

Josiah whirled around to see Hope claw her hands into the ground beside him at the pit. Her body shook as she cried again, "Stop!"

They did, and Silas elbowed his way out from under the pile and got to his feet.

"Tell your brother I wasn't there—holding the knife to your throat!" he said to Hope. "Tell him I wasn't there!"

"No, you weren't," Hope said, her voice shivering. "But you knew about it, didn't you? *Didn't you?*"

"Aye! They told me later, but—"

"Did they tell you they held that knife at my throat for hours, making me think they were surely going to kill me?"

"Aye, but—"

"But you did nothing about it."

"I did!"

"Liar!" Hope cried.

Silas shook his head furiously. "They've never attacked you again, have they? Nay, because I took Jonathon's knife!"

The three Putnam cousins turned to statues, and Silas closed his eyes as if he knew he had just made a terrible mistake.

"Did they also tell you they would do something horrible to me or my family or our property if I told what they'd done?" Hope said.

Josiah looked at her sharply.

"Aye, they did," Silas said.

"Then was it you who came back and untied my feet so I could at least run away?" she asked.

Silas didn't answer.

"Well, was it you?" Hope said again.

Silas shook his head, and Hope looked wildly at Josiah. "And you want to forgive *that?*" she screamed at him.

"I just don't want you to be afraid like this forever!" Josiah said. "If you never forgive, you're always alone—and scared."

The words had sounded so strong and right coming out

of Joseph Putnam's mouth. Now, they sounded weak and cowardly.

"Where is it now, cousin?" Jonathon suddenly shouted. "Where is my knife now?"

Silas could only stammer.

"You never took it!" Jonathon said. "You only lied to get yourself out of this pit—and you're naught but a brainless ninny!"

"I did. Here, you can see it!"

Josiah watched in horror as Silas reached under his vest and yanked out the knife. Even in the darkness, the blade gleamed as Josiah had seen it do once before. With one angry lunge, Jonathon snatched the knife from Silas, plunged it into the side of the pit, and hoisted himself up by it. Wildly, Josiah grabbed Hope's arm.

"Run!" he shouted. "Run with her north, Sarah!" He jabbed his finger into the air to the south. "Run as fast as you can!"

Sarah clamped her fingers around Hope's sleeve and dragged her south. "Get the bag!" Josiah cried to William. William dove behind the bushes and came out with the cloth sack, which he tossed to Josiah. Jonathon was already clawing his way to the top of the pit when Josiah dumped a load of long grass from the Hutchinson swamp into his face.

"Go!" Josiah called to William, and together they tore south, crashing through the bushes at the base of Thorndike Hill. He knew the grass would stop Jonathon only for as long as it would take to paw his way out from underneath it. And then he would be on them—with his knife.

William suddenly skidded to a stop. "What was that?" he said.

"What?" Josiah said. "Come on."

"No, it sounded like a hammer! Listen!"

William jerked Josiah behind a tree, and they listened. There it was—the unmistakable sound of a hammer driving a stake into the ground. A moment later, it came again.

Jonathon began to scream—still from the pit.

"What in the name of—?"

"What is it?" they heard Eleazer shout.

"A net, idiot! You there, get this off!" There was more pounding from the hammer, and then another voice laughed into the night. "Not in a million years!" it cried. "Not in a million years!"

Josiah stared at William, whose eyes were as big as two pewter plates. He'd recognized it, too. It was the voice of Ezekiel Porter.

"Cut the net with your knife, Jonathon!" Richard Putnam cried out.

"I'm cutting as fast as I can!" Jonathon shouted back.

But Josiah leaned forward to listen for Ezekiel's voice again. Had he actually been there, hammering a net over the opening to the pit?

And then still another voice came, this time a girl's, whispering to them from the bottom of the hill.

"Josiah! William!" she said hoarsely. "Run to our barn! It's safe there!"

"It's Rachel Porter!" William said. He brought his face close to Josiah's in the darkness. "I don't care if you trust the Porters or not, I'm going there."

"Aye, I'm with you!" Josiah said, and he scrambled behind William through the underbrush on hands and knees until they reached the road. It wouldn't take Jonathon Putnam long to tear his knife through a net, angry as he was. Josiah wanted to be well out of the way to avoid meeting the same blade face-to-face.

They ran all the way to Hadlock's Bridge and then cut over toward the Porters' barn. A faint light glowed through the crack in the door, and when Josiah and William slipped inside, they found Sarah and Hope already huddled next to the lamp.

"Rachel jumped out of the bushes and nearly scared us out of our wits!" Sarah said. "She told us to come here."

"Us, too," William said.

"The grass worked then. You got away."

The door creaked open.

"'Twas no grass kept them in that pit," a breathless Rachel Porter said smugly. "'Twas a net."

"A net?" said William.

"But where did it come from?" added Josiah.

"Did Ezekiel do it?"

"Ezekiel?"

"Aye, Ezekiel!" Ezekiel grinned at them as he slithered in.

Hope sat up straight in Sarah's arms. "Are they coming?" she whispered between her teeth. "Did they follow you?"

"Follow me?" Ezekiel gave a short, satisfied laugh. "They'll be some time cutting their way out of that net, eh, Rachel?"

Rachel nodded and smiled triumphantly as she pulled back Hope's cap and smoothed her hand over her dark hair. "You've naught to worry about them, Hope."

Hope looked warily at all of them, and Josiah shook his head in confusion.

"I don't understand," he said.

"When we heard what your plan was, we knew it wouldn't work unless you had some way of keeping the Putnams in the trap," Ezekiel said.

Rachel nodded. "Just in case they didn't agree to your offer . . . which they didn't."

"But how did you hear our plan?" Sarah said.

"And where did you get a net?" William put in.

"Start from the beginning, Ezekiel," Rachel said. She wiggled her eyebrows at the rest of them. "You shall *love* this story!"

But to Josiah's surprise, Ezekiel didn't plunge immediately into the tale. Instead, he looked sideways at Josiah. "Perhaps Josiah doesn't want to hear it," he said. "He doesn't believe a thing I say, you know."

"Oh, don't be a ninny! Tell it!" Rachel commanded.

Josiah swallowed hard. "Aye," he said. "I want to hear."

Ezekiel gave him one last look, and then his eyes grew wide as he began to talk.

"The Putnams went too far this time. I knew sooner or later you'd need some help. So I started to follow you—Josiah and William—just sometimes, when you didn't know I was there. When I saw you, Josiah, talking to Joseph Putnam so seriously out on the road that one evening, I thought to ask him if you were in trouble. He said I might want to eavesdrop on a meeting you were having, up at the Blessing Place."

Sarah gasped and covered her mouth with her hand. "You spied on us?"

"He's not some ward of the devil, Sarah," Rachel said. "And lucky for you he did, too."

"As I said, I knew you were going to need some way to keep the Putnams trapped until you could get away, just in case—"

"But the net," William said impatiently. "Where did you get it?"

Ezekiel looked slyly at Rachel. "We made it."

"The two of you made a net?" Sarah said. "How did you know how?"

"It isn't exactly a net," Ezekiel said. He looked at Josiah. "Remember the day you came to visit my grandfather and we were tightening the ropes under his bed? That was naught but a net made of thick rope. When he died, they put his bed here in the barn and everyone forgot about it."

"Except us," Rachel said. "It took us only one night to turn it into the finishing touch for your bear trap."

Ezekiel burned his big eyes right into Josiah's. "I'm not a coward then, am I, Josiah Hutchinson? And I wasn't a coward the day I made the Putnams think there was a bear nearby so you and that baby girl could get away from them."

"That was you?" Josiah said.

Ezekiel gave a crooked smile. "Aye. I told you I would prove it to you. Have I?"

Josiah nodded and looked down at the toes of his boots, where bits of underbrush stuck out of the soles. There was more he needed to say, and once again, Joseph Putnam's words were right there in his thoughts, crowding out everything else. But would they sound cowardly again?

There was an awkward silence. Josiah could feel his eyes wanting to look everywhere but into Ezekiel's. He wished he could run from the barn and come back tomorrow and pretend he and Ezekiel had never been mad at each other to begin with.

"I have a question," Hope said. "Ezekiel, how did you know the Putnams had gone too far this time? I never told anyone—not even Josiah."

It was Ezekiel's turn to look awkward. His gaze fumbled down toward his hands as he said, "I was near the widow's cabin that day when they came out laughing, those three Putnams, bragging about how they had scared 'that Hutchinson girl.' And I heard you crying inside when they left."

"Then it was you!" Hope said. She pawed at Ezekiel's arm. "It was you who came in and untied my feet!"

Ezekiel nodded.

"Why did you not untie my hands and take away my blind-fold?" she said. "Why didn't you tell me who you were?"

Josiah leaned forward. He wanted to know the same thing.

"I knew you would find a way to get loose, once you could walk," Ezekiel said, shifting his feet uneasily.

Josiah watched him carefully, but Ezekiel wouldn't look at him.

"It doesn't matter," Rachel said. "Hope is safe. You're all safe."

"And we haven't really solved anything," Josiah said.

Everyone looked at him, and the victorious expressions slid off of their faces.

Sarah sighed heavily. "Why did we ever think the Putnams would agree to end the war just to keep us from telling on them? Who would believe us anyway?"

"That plan worked for them," Hope said. All eyes turned to her.

"What do you mean?" Rachel said.

"It wasn't just their threats that frightened me into not telling anyone," she said. "Even when they chopped down the widow's cabin—and I knew that was a warning—I didn't tell because it was my word against theirs. This would be the same thing. Some people would believe them and some would believe me, and there would be no end to it because there were no witnesses."

Josiah's heart lurched. "There was one," he said. "One who didn't really want to be a witness, so he didn't reveal himself."

Their gazes followed his. Ezekiel looked back sharply. "You can't call me a witness. I didn't actually see them put the knife to her throat." Ezekiel's eyes shifted.

"But you were *there!*" Sarah said.

"Isn't it enough that I saved her?" his voice cracked. "Isn't it enough that I saved all of you tonight? You want me to speak out against the Putnams, too? I've done enough, Josiah!"

Suddenly, all the meaning of Joseph Putnam's words rushed into Josiah's head. He put his face close to Ezekiel's.

"You didn't have to do any of it," Josiah said. "I forgive you no matter what. You wouldn't be speaking out against the Putnams to prove you're brave. You'd be doing it so none of us would have to be afraid anymore."

Josiah rocked back on his heels and watched Ezekiel, whose eyes thrashed around, searching for someone who was on his side. No one looked back.

"I don't know," he said finally. "I don't think I can do that—alone."

"You wouldn't be alone, Ezekiel," Hope said. Her voice held the first brightness that Josiah had heard in it for weeks. "I'd be with you."

"We would all be with you," William said. He poked his sister. "Wouldn't we?"

"Aye," Sarah said faintly.

"See?" Ezekiel cried. "She's scared. You're all scared!"

"My father's scared, too, but he does what's right!" Josiah blurted out.

They all stared at him. At some point, he'd gotten to his feet, and he knew his face was red and his arms were waving madly.

"All the men are scared," he shouted at Ezekiel. "But they go to each other—they go to God—and then they do what has to be done. If we don't do that, we'll always be fighting with the Putnams, and we'll always be scared!"

Ezekiel looked back at Josiah with doubtful eyes. Josiah let his arms flop to his sides.

"We have to go now, Hope," he said in a voice even he barely heard. "We have to get Dorcas from Betty Parris."

And then he turned and left the barn.

✞ ✞ ✞

either Josiah nor Hope spoke a word as they trudged across the road from the parsonage with Dorcas sleeping on Josiah's back. There was nothing to say as far as Josiah could see, because after all they had been through, nothing had changed.

He and Ezekiel were still mad at each other. Hope was still looking over her shoulder, trembling over what might be coming up behind her. The Putnams were still out there somewhere, waiting for a chance to get back at them.

As if to prove it, a familiar tall shape stepped out from behind the bush that stood at the corner of the Hutchinsons' property. Hope slammed into Josiah's side and gasped.

Oh, God, please, Josiah prayed for at least the hundredth time that night. *Please help*.

"You think you're clever, don't you, Hutchinson?" Jonathon Putnam said.

Dorcas whimpered in her sleep and Hope clung to his arm, but Josiah kept walking, trying to edge past. Jonathon

185

blocked his way and walked backward, his eyes boring down on them in the darkness.

"Where do you think you're going?" he said.

"To my house," Josiah answered. "This is our property you're on now." He could feel Hope's fingers squeezing into his flesh.

"I don't care where we are, Hutchinson. Let us be in the middle of the Meeting House with Reverend Parris himself looking on—I will make you pay for what you did tonight!"

Before Josiah could take another step, Jonathon's hand shot under his vest and came out with the knife. Hope pierced the air with a scream.

"She's afraid of my knife," Jonathon said, his eyes burning with a glint that matched his blade. "And if you've any sense, boy, you will be, too."

"Josiah!" Hope screamed again.

Dorcas wrenched awake and began to cry. Hope clawed at his back and kept screaming, "Josiah! *Jo-siah!*"

God, please help us! was all Josiah could think. He stared, motionless, at the knife in Jonathon Putnam's hand.

"You said we were even," Jonathon spat through his teeth. "But we will never be even, Hutchinson. Not so long as I can put that fear in your eyes."

He pulled the knife up to his shoulder so its vicious point loomed over Josiah's head. Josiah followed it with his eyes—and saw the movement behind Jonathon, past his shoulder, at the front door of the Hutchinsons' house.

"Papa!" Josiah screamed. "Papa, help! Help us!"

It was as if his call opened a gate and let out a whole herd of voices: Hope screaming behind him, Dorcas sobbing in his ear,

Jonathon hurling threats into his face . . . and a knot of angry men running toward them, filling the air with their shouts.

"Josiah, what is it?" shouted Papa. "What's wrong?"

"The boy's taken leave of his senses, Hutchinson!" Thomas Putnam cried.

"Aye!" Nathaniel Putnam piped up.

"Good heavens, Joseph, that boy has a knife." The last words came from Joseph Putnam. Papa's big hand came up and snatched the blade from Jonathon's grasp. Suddenly, there was silence. Even Thomas Putnam had nothing to say. There was only the crying from Hope and Dorcas, and Josiah's heart pounding out of his chest.

Finally, Nathaniel Putnam spoke. "There must be some reason, some explanation . . . "

"I care not for explanations, Putnam," Papa said to Nathaniel. Josiah didn't think he'd ever heard his father's voice so angry. "I told your brother once that if he or any of his brood ever laid a hand on one of my family members, only God would have mercy on him. The same goes for you, Nathaniel."

"Did you touch him, Jonathon?" Nathaniel said, his words screeching over his son like fingernails on a slate.

"Nay," Jonathon said.

"Then take your threats elsewhere, Hutchinson," Nathaniel said. He took hold of Jonathon's arm as if to pull him away, but Joseph Hutchinson stopped them both with his words.

"What were you doing with a knife, boy, if you didn't intend to use it?"

"He never intended to use it, Papa. He only likes to scare

people with it." Six pairs of surprised eyes turned on Hope.
"He's naught but a coward," she said.

Her eyelids were so swollen that they were nearly shut,
and tears continued to track down her goose-colored cheeks,
but even in the darkness Josiah saw a spark coming from her
eyes.

"Are you telling me the truth, Hope?" Goodman
Hutchinson said. "You're not dissembling for fear of what this
boy might do to you later?"

Hope tossed her head. "No, Papa."

"And you, Josiah?"

Josiah could feel Hope poking him in the back, and he
spoke slowly. "He makes people think he's going to hurt them
with his knife. Scares them out of their senses so they don't
even know who they are."

Papa's eyes scrutinized Josiah. He turned his gaze to
Nathaniel Putnam and gave him the same scrutinzing look. "I
would be ashamed to call such a sniveling coward my son," he
said. "Get him off my land."

"Now see here—" Thomas Putnam cut in.

"You go as well, Thomas," Papa said tightly. "And remember my words to you—if your brood of vipers lays one hand on
anyone living under my roof, may God Himself have mercy on
your soul."

Thomas Putnam sputtered and then turned to march away
as if he'd just won some triumphant victory. Nathaniel, too,
moved off, his hand around Jonathon's arm, but he stopped
and held out his other palm toward Joseph Hutchinson.

"What?" Papa said.

"The knife, if you please."

Papa's face contorted into a question mark. "Have you gone daft, Putnam? I'll not put this weapon back into that boy's hands!"

"You're putting it in my hands!"

"Ach! And how long before he's carrying it again, eh, Putnam? And why shouldn't he? You set the example yourself by toting a musket and pulling it on your neighbors."

"You have no right to keep that weapon, Hutchinson!" Nathaniel whined. "It belongs to me!"

Papa's eyebrows shot up to his hairline, and Joseph Putnam shook his head in disbelief.

"Does it, now?" Papa said quietly. "Then either your son stole it from you or you gave it to him. In either case, you are not to be trusted with it, as I see it."

"Aye," Joseph Putnam said softly.

All three of the other Putnam faces glowed crimson in the darkness. Thomas raised his fist.

"May God Himself have mercy on your soul," Papa said firmly.

Within a minute, the Putnams had disappeared down the road. As if in relief, Dorcas let out a long, agonized whimper.

"Well, Little Papa," Josiah's father said. "You'd best get that child inside to her mother."

"Her mother!" Hope cried.

"Deliverance Carrier? Here?" Josiah said.

"You convinced them to let her go?"

"How? When?"

"Ach!" Papa put his hand up for silence as Joseph Putnam chuckled softly beside him. "We'll sort this all out inside, and I'll be wanting an explanation for why all three of you were traipsing about the countryside in the middle of the night."

He turned toward the house, and Hope nudged Josiah's ribs. "Let me do the talking," she said.

Josiah agreed. He would have agreed to anything, because the old Hope was back.

Dorcas plastered her arms so hard around his neck, Josiah thought she would strangle him—until they walked into the Hutchinson kitchen and she saw her mother by the hearth. Deliverance nearly tossed her trencher of porridge aside bolting from her stool, and Dorcas lunged over Josiah's shoulder right into her mother's arms. Deliverance kissed her so many times that Josiah slunk down at the table to study his boot tops.

"Here, Josiah," Mama said into his ear. She slipped a bowl of syrup-covered bread in front of him. "This will keep your mind occupied."

"Your papa is a fine man," Deliverance said. She scooped Dorcas's face into her neck. "He saved my life today."

"Ach, you'd not have been hanged, Deliverance," Papa said, waving her off with one of his big hands.

"But I'd have died in the jail sure, if it hadn't been for ye."

"Will you tell us the story, Papa?" Hope said.

Goodman Hutchinson ran a hand over his face. "There's naught to tell. God was merciful, and so was the court."

"He's far too modest, Hope," Joseph Putnam said. "So with your permission, Joseph, I'll tell your children what kind of man you are, eh?"

Papa shrugged and took the cup of cider Deborah

Hutchinson handed him. Josiah set his spoon down and listened.

"Your father went before the Essex County magistrates this morning, and he waited for nearly two hours while Nathaniel Putnam went on about the travesty that had been done to him by this vicious woman, who had not only trespassed on his property but had taken up residence there with the intent to claim it as her own. Putnam brought in maps and depositions the likes of which you've never seen."

Josiah was sure of that, although he didn't even know what a deposition was.

"By the time Nathaniel Putnam was finished, the magistrates were all nodding their heads and looking at your father as if to say, 'The facts seem clear. What are you doing here, man?'" Joseph Putnam smiled. "And then it was your papa's turn. He had no maps of Salem Village or statements about Goody Carrier's character. He had only God's thoughts and his own words to put them into. He said he didn't think Deliverance Carrier was the one who should be on trial. He said it was the village itself."

Joseph Putnam's eyes twinkled, and he paused a moment to nurture the suspense. "You can imagine the flurry that stirred up in the courtroom! The Putnams all huffed and puffed, but one of the magistrates pounded his table for silence and asked what he meant by that. Your father reminded them that the Puritan people—our fathers—came to this new world to live according to the teachings of Jesus Christ and no other. He pointed out that Jesus Himself told us to be Good Samaritans, to feed His sheep, no matter how poor. And yet, your papa explained, it was obvious that was not happening, because Deliverance Carrier, through no fault of her own, was forced to go out begging. And when no one would give her so much as a crust of bread, she even had to steal a piece of land for a night so she could rest enough to start again the next day. Then your father looked them all in the eye and said the only person in the village of Salem who should not be jailed for what happened to Deliverance Carrier was his own son, Josiah Hutchinson. Josiah Hutchinson had reached out and tried to help her, and when she disappeared and left her child in his care, he went out to try to find her."

Josiah squirmed in his seat.

"He said that in court?" Hope asked.

Joseph Putnam nodded proudly. "Aye, he did. He told them that if every person in Salem Village were as much of a true Christian as his son, there would be no poor people to drag into the courts. He asked permission to show his own Christian virtue by being allowed to pay Deliverance's fines and keep her in his care until he could get her to her kinsmen in Marblehead." Joseph Putnam took a deep breath. "And the court refused."

Josiah's spoon clattered to the plate. "Refused!"

"Aye, they would not let your father pay Goody Carrier's fines . . . because there were no fines."

Josiah's father chuckled and said, "I wish you children could have seen the faces of Nathaniel and Thomas Putnam when those words were spoken. Poor Thomas's head nearly flew from his shoulders."

Joseph Putnam smiled. "So the matter was dismissed, and the magistrates admonished everyone to spend more time practicing their faith and less time hauling their neighbors into court." He nodded his handsome head toward Goodman Hutchinson. "Your father saved more than one life today, I'll warrant you."

There was a reverent silence, which Hope broke timidly. "Papa?" she said.

Papa's eyes rested easily on his daughter. "Speak, child," he said.

"I know you want to know where we were tonight."

"Aye."

"We shall tell you, but before we do, I want to say that what you said in court is right. Josiah is a true Christian man. And what he did tonight he did because he is."

Goodman Hutchinson turned his brooding, hooded eyes on Josiah and let them gaze there until Josiah could barely look back any longer.

"Good, then," Papa said finally. "That is all I need to know. You need tell me no more."

Deliverance Carrier was sent upstairs to sleep in Hope and Josiah's room with Dorcas, and Hope and Josiah spread quilts on the settles by the fire in the kitchen for themselves. The footsteps had hardly died on the stairs above them before Hope scrambled off of her settle and joined Josiah on his.

"I could say you were a stupid boy tonight, Josiah," she said, "to try to win the Putnams over like that."

"A few minutes ago, I was a brave Christian man!"

"You are. That's why I'm not going to say you were stupid."

Josiah shook his head. This was all too confusing for a mind that had seen so much in one night.

"I just want to know one thing," she said.

Josiah sighed and rubbed his eyes. "What?"

"Does it really make a difference?"

"Does *what* make a difference?"

"Forgiving."

Josiah stopped rubbing and thought. He'd forgiven a lot of people tonight. All the Putnam cousins. Ezekiel. Maybe even himself. Still, on the way home, it had seemed that things were just the same as ever. But were they?

It looked as if at least one of the Putnams—Silas—might have some good in him.

Josiah didn't hate Ezekiel anymore. He just felt sorry for him now because he was still locked up in some kind of fearful cage.

And Jonathon Putnam had been revealed as the coward he was. He only wanted people to think he was dangerous.

Besides all that, Josiah just didn't feel alone anymore. Hope was sitting on the settle beside him, nagging him like she always used to. Papa trusted him enough not to ask questions about what he had been doing all evening.

Maybe everything wasn't perfect, but some things were different now. They were better.

"Aye," he said to Hope. "Forgiving does make a difference." He yawned. "I wish I'd done it a long time ago."

He stretched out on the warm spot she left on the settle as she moved to her own place. He was asleep almost before she got there—but not before he heard her whisper, "I wish I had, too."

✝ ✝ ✝

Chapter Twenty

The next day, Papa took Deliverance to Marblehead in the wagon to see if her husband's relatives would take her and Dorcas in for a time.

"Just so long as it takes for me to find my own way again," Deliverance told Papa firmly.

Dorcas screamed when her mother left until Deborah Hutchinson said, "Josiah, leave your chores for the moment and see to her. She has always loved you best."

"I won't miss this at all," Josiah mumbled under his breath, as Dorcas toddled happily after him across the yard. He stopped and looked over at the parsonage. "But I know someone who will."

"Where are you going, Josiah?" Hope called to him from the kitchen window.

"To Betty Parris's," Josiah called back.

"Wait. I want to go with you."

Betty's pale eyes grew the size of kettles when she saw Hope with Josiah in the bushes.

"Don't be afraid," Hope said. "I came to thank you for your part in the plan to stop the war. You were very brave."

Betty pulled the chirping Dorcas into her arms and hugged her. "Did it work?" she said.

"No," said Josiah.

"Well, not yet," Hope cut in. "But we haven't given up yet. That's why I need a favor from you."

Josiah stared at her. But Betty leaned in, her eyes all shimmery. He would never understand girls.

"Josiah tells me you have beautiful handwriting and lots of paper."

"Aye, my papa gives me the scraps when he's finished writing his sermons," Betty said. "He's the one who taught me how to write. In fact, I have something for Dorcas." She pulled a tiny piece of parchment from her sleeve and tucked it into Josiah's hand. "Will you give it to her when she leaves?" she said sadly.

Josiah put the piece of paper into the pouch inside his breeches.

"Will you write a message for me, like you did for Josiah?" Hope said. "And see that it's delivered?"

"Aye!" Betty said. Her thin face lit up like a sunrise. "Tituba will help me."

"Good. Please write a message to Jonathon Putnam—"

"Jonathon Putnam!" Josiah said.

"Hush, Josiah, just listen," Hope said. "Tell him that we have a witness," she said to Betty, "and if they attack us again, our witness will talk. We have forgiven. The war is over."

Josiah watched as Betty mouthed the message, but his mind was racing over Hope's words.

"Our witness will talk?" he said to his sister as they hurried away with Dorcas in tow. "Ezekiel never agreed to that!"

"I've done my part, Josiah," she said. "This part's up to you."

"But—"

Calmly, she put out her arms to take Dorcas. "You were right, you know. It does make a difference when you forgive."

Josiah was so busy catching up on his farmwork that he didn't know until suppertime that his father and Deliverance had returned from Marblehead. He saw the wagon at the barn, but before he could get to the kitchen to learn the news, he heard voices from the best room. Although the door was closed, he could feel the heat rising. He would have thought it was the Putnams back again if he hadn't known those tones so well. Those were Porter voices he heard.

"Do you deny it, Giles?" Papa said on the other side of the door. "Do you deny that you are now openly asking me to take part in a plot to drive Reverend Parris from the church?"

"A plot, Joseph?" Giles laughed, and Josiah could almost see his charming smile flashing across the best room at Papa. "You make it sound like the work of the devil!"

"Is it?" Josiah's father said. "Because if it is, I'll have no part in it. I only agreed to come back to the church in the village to see if I could turn the hearts of some of these stiff-necked people by showing them that I support the Lord's work. I promised your grandfather that I would do that. I knew nothing of a scheme to use the property my father gave to the church to bring that same church to ruin. And now you are openly asking me—"

"Joseph—" Benjamin Porter said, a little nervously.

"That is what you and this boy are asking me to do, Benjamin, and I'll have none of it."

"Joseph, please, be calm," Giles said. His voice was as smooth as a snakeskin, and Josiah shivered at the sound of it. "Now hear me out," he went on. "You will agree that the Putnams have nearly taken control of the church, Reverend Parris included. They have convinced him that they are the sole reason he was selected to come here when your father and my grandfather opposed it. You will agree?"

Papa grunted.

"And you will also agree," Giles continued, "that those same Putnams are an evil lot. You've seen it yourself in this situation with the beggar woman. They are not interested in doing the Lord's work. They're only interested in having power, and they are using the church to get that power because they have failed so miserably as farmers. You will grant me that, Joseph?"

"Aye, but—"

"Let me finish, if you will. If we are to have a church left at all, we have no choice remaining but to replace this evil influence with one that is of God."

There was a slamming sound, and Josiah knew his father had pounded his fist on the table. Josiah retreated under the steps and waited.

"Replace them?" Papa thundered. "I never agreed to try to replace them. My intent was to try to *change* them. And I have come to the conclusion that that cannot be done."

"Then we must take the next step."

"Which is what, Giles? What, Benjamin? To drive out the

minister and most of his flock by pulling the very church buildings from under them, in the name of God?"

"If that's what it takes," Giles said. "And then we begin again—fresh."

"No!" The ceiling shook with Goodman Hutchinson's answer. "I did not know this was your plan, Giles. You continually denied it, even at your own grandfather's funeral, when you showed me the agreement the Putnams had with Mr. Parris to sign the land over to him. I said I would hate to see that, but I never said I wanted the land back. If I had known this was in your mind, I never would have set foot in that church again. Samuel Parris may be a timid, whining man, but if I wanted him out of his pulpit, I would have said so to his face. It may be that I am on his side in this, though, boy. The poor man has much more going against him than he knows."

Josiah could tell the conversation was coming to a close, and he slipped silently into the kitchen.

"We'll need more wood for supper, Josiah," Mama said. "It's to be a celebration tonight. Deliverance and Dorcas's family have agreed to take them in."

But Josiah didn't answer as he turned and went slowly to the woodpile. "If I had known," Papa had said to Giles. *Papa could have known*, Josiah thought, *if I'd told him what I heard from under the table at Israel Porter's funeral*. Josiah shook his head. That was back when he'd tried to do everything himself. He couldn't make that mistake anymore.

After supper, Josiah made his way toward the Porter farm. Since spring was slipping into summer, there was no chill in the air, just the softness that promised days full of blackberries and evenings full of fireflies. But Josiah's thoughts were serious. If he couldn't work out all the things that nagged at his mind, summer wasn't going to be any fun at all. Nothing was.

Rachel was sitting on the front step with her needlework when he arrived, and she eyed him suspiciously.

"Ezekiel's down by the river," she said. "But if you've come to place more blame on him, Josiah Hutchinson, you'd best just turn around and go back the way you came. He has saved you several times over already. I don't know what more you want from him."

Josiah didn't answer but turned wearily toward the Frost Fish River, which ran behind the Porters' property down to the sawmill.

He heard the plopping before he saw Ezekiel, and he knew he was skimming stones across the water. At first, Josiah didn't say anything; he just picked up a handful of rocks and pelted a few easily across the top of the water.

"Thanks for savin' us last night," Josiah said finally. "If you hadn't been there with that net, we'd have been in the Putnams' hands sure."

Ezekiel shrugged.

"I'm grateful to you for that day in the church, too, when you told the deacon I was afear'd of snakes. And when you ran the Putnams off by pretendin' to be a bear. And for helpin' Hope escape, too. There's a lot of good in you, Ezekiel."

"Aye, there is," Ezekiel said tightly. "I'm glad you finally see it."

Josiah skimmed a stone across the top of the water. "You did it all by yourself, too, without anybody knowing."

At that Ezekiel grunted. Josiah took a deep breath. Now came the hard part.

"But there might come a time when people will have to know, Ezekiel."

Ezekiel looked at him sharply. "Know what?"

"That you saw the Putnams come out of the widow's cabin, and when you went in, Hope was tied up."

"And then they'll come after *me!*"

"No, they won't." Josiah set the rest of his stones down on the mud and stepped toward Ezekiel. "You might never have to tell anyone. If they know we have a witness, the Putnams will probably never do another thing to us. You would only have to tell if they started the war up again."

"You know they will! Those Putnams are evil, Josiah, right to the center of their souls!"

"I don't think anybody's *all* bad."

"Ha!"

"Look at Betty Parris helping us with Dorcas! Look at Silas Putnam taking Jonathon's knife! Even you, Ezekiel. Look at you."

Ezekiel cut him a sideways glance. "What about me?"

"You're bad . . . but you're not *all* bad."

"Mongrel!" Ezekiel said. "Take that back!"

Josiah grinned. "I'll fight you for it."

"You'll never win, Josiah Hutchinson!" Ezekiel cried. But Josiah caught the shine in his eyes as he hurled himself at Josiah's shoulders, and the two of them tumbled down the slope like two bear cubs.

"Say I'm not bad at all, mongrel," Ezekiel said when he had Josiah pinned.

"Half bad, half good!" Josiah said and rolled him over on his back.

At that moment, a familiar, menacing voice called out. "Look at that, Eleazer. Now they've turned on each other!"

Both Josiah and Ezekiel froze and jerked their faces toward the top of the riverbank. Jonathon Putnam stood smirking down at them with Eleazer matching him smirk for smirk.

Josiah scrambled to his feet, but Jonathon put up a long-fingered hand. "You've naught to go running away like a coward, Hutchinson. I only have a question for you."

Josiah watched cautiously as Jonathon reached inside his vest. Was there another knife? But Jonathon pulled out a piece of parchment and waved it toward him.

"I got this today," he said, still smirking, "a message from you, saying you have a witness who can prove 'twas us who held your sister hostage."

"Aye," Josiah said slowly. He didn't dare look at Ezekiel. He could feel him turning to stone beside him.

"So here is my question, Hutchinson. Who is this so-called witness, eh?"

Josiah didn't answer, and he still didn't look at Ezekiel. If he had only had more time to talk to Ezekiel and convince him to promise to come forward if he had to. Now they were right back where they started.

"It is just as I thought, Eleazer," Jonathon said, his lip curling nearly to his nose. "The Hutchinsons and Porters talk big, but they're naught but cowards. All of them!"

"It's me, Jonathon!" Ezekiel burst out. "I'm the witness."

Jonathon stared at him for a moment before he snorted.

"Ha! You're a liar as well as a coward."

"I am no liar."

Josiah stole a glance at Ezekiel. His pointy cheekbones nearly poked from under his skin, and his eyes were in angry slits. "I was there, outside the widow's cabin, when you came out bragging and waving your knife. I went in, and Hope Hutchinson was there, tied and blindfolded and cryin' her eyes out. I know what you did, Jonathon Putnam, because I was there. I am no liar." Ezekiel took a step forward. "And I'm no coward either. Don't ever call me or any of my friends that again."

Jonathon gave a short, hard laugh, but Josiah could see there were questions in his eyes. "You talk big now, when there are no adults about. But would you say this to . . . my father, perhaps? Or my uncle Thomas? Or perhaps in front of the magistrates in Salem Town?"

Ezekiel glanced anxiously at Josiah. Josiah gave him a tiny nod.

"Just as I thought," Jonathon said. "You never would—"

"Aye, I would," Ezekiel said. His voice was tiny, but the words were there.

"What's that, *boy?*" Jonathon said.

"I said I would tell—anyone," Ezekiel said. He glanced once more at Josiah. "My friends would stand behind me, too."

"I don't believe you," Jonathon said. But something in his eyes told Josiah that part of him did. His shoulders went up like hackles on a dog. "We'll just see," he said.

"Yes, we shall," Ezekiel said. "Because if you do one more evil thing to the Proctors or the Hutchinsons or the Porters—to anyone—I'll tell."

Josiah smothered a smile. Ezekiel had folded his arms across his chest, and his head was cocked to one side. He was enjoying himself now.

"We'll just see," Jonathon said again, and, hackles still up, he pulled Eleazer up the bank with him. They both hurried off a little faster than they needed to.

"You did it," Josiah whispered to Ezekiel when they were gone.

"It was nothing," Ezekiel said, swaggering back toward the river. But Josiah caught the tears that shimmered in his eyes, and he gave him a minute to swallow them before he wrapped himself around him and wrestled him to the ground again.

Two days later, Joseph Hutchinson took Deliverance and Dorcas to Marblehead and asked Josiah to go along. "I should never get down the road without that baby screaming for you," his father said to him as they hitched up the oxen to the wagon.

"Why did she have to choose me?" Josiah muttered.

"Because children have a way of seein' the good in people," Papa said. "And you have a great deal of good in you, Josiah. A great deal more than most of the other men in this village, I daresay."

Josiah's eyes went to the ground, but his father reached down and pulled his chin up with his fingers. "Don't ever be ashamed of being a good man, son. It means you're close to God, and He's close to you."

Josiah watched as his father climbed into the wagon, his thoughts already elsewhere. Of course, Papa was right. God felt closer than He had for a long time.

When they arrived in Marblehead, Deliverance said to Dorcas, "The boy must go, child. Ye have to turn loose of him now."

But Dorcas only clamped her arms more firmly around Josiah's neck. Josiah looked helplessly at his father, who simply smiled and turned to Deliverance.

"You should be safe here in Marblehead with your husband's people. They seem a decent sort."

"I can never repay ye," Deliverance said in her raspy voice. She clawed her skirts and chewed at her lip.

"I was only doing God's work," Papa said. "So set your sights on repayin' Him, eh?"

Deliverance looked at Josiah. "I never set much store by God after the way I've been treated by the people who claim to be His children, but I've seen somethin' different in ye Hutchinsons—all of ye."

Josiah peeled Dorcas's arms away, and she started to whimper. Again, his eyes pleaded with his father.

"Do something quick," Papa said with a rare twinkle in his eye. "We must be on our way."

Josiah set Dorcas on the ground, where she wailed, "'Siah!"

"Hush now," Josiah said. But of course she didn't. He rubbed his hands up and down the legs of his breeches, and then he felt it—the piece of paper Betty Parris had given him to pass on to Dorcas.

"Here," he said, digging it out. "'Tis a special message for you."

She stopped crying immediately and stuck out her now chubby hands for the piece of parchment. As she puckered her tiny brows over the message, Josiah practically ran to the wagon. But a frail, hopeful little voice stopped him.

"'Siah?" she said.

He turned to see her holding out the paper, her forehead bunched up.

"Ye'd better tell her what it says," Deliverance said. "I can't read."

Josiah took the paper from her and squatted down. On it, Betty had drawn a tiny figure with fluffy wings and wispy hair like Dorcas's. Below it, the round, neat handwriting said, "Yer Angl."

"What is it?" Papa called from the wagon.

"'Your Angel,'" Josiah muttered to Dorcas.

She stared at it for longer than Josiah could stay there. He got up quickly, and this time he made it all the way to the wagon before she called out to him again.

"*You* angel!" she said in her chirpy voice, pointing a pink finger at him.

"Can we go, please, Papa?" Josiah said.

Papa chuckled and clicked his tongue at the oxen. But as they moved off, Josiah sneaked one more glance back at Dorcas. She was clutching her paper and waving, with tiny tears glistening in her eyes. As he waved back, there was a pang in his chest.

They were nearly back to Salem Village before Papa interrupted his thoughts. "So you're an angel, now, eh?" he said. The wrinkles played merrily around his eyes.

Josiah shrugged and wished he could shake off the red glow that was creeping up his cheeks.

"Well, I'd say that was somewhat correct," his father went on. "You've been something of an angel of mercy of late."

Josiah mumbled a "thank you" and tried not to look down at his boots.

Joseph Hutchinson cleared his throat. "You've tried to do far too much on your own, and I was bent on chiding you for that. But I've given it some thought and some prayer, and I've discovered that the people who should be teaching you how to be a man are not doing much of a job of it." Papa twitched his shoulders. "Our fathers came to this new place to live in community. It's the church community who should be teaching its young how to work together, but this church has given you no example to go by. These people can no longer even see the good in each other, and I fear they're falling away from God."

He gave Josiah a long look and then continued. "There is hatred in our midst, Josiah. The very people we should be able to trust and work beside refuse to ever soften and forgive. I fear God's people in Salem Village are in trouble, and I no longer see what I can do to change that. You mustn't be surprised, son, if someday soon our family—"

But he stopped there, and Josiah followed his startled gaze. They had pulled up beside the sawmill, and Josiah saw at once what sent his father hurtling from the wagon. The walkway that led to the entrance had been chopped away and its wooden planks left in splinters. A picture of the widow's cabin, lying in ruins at the edge of the woods, seared into Josiah's mind.

"This was no accident," Papa said. The network of lines on his cheeks began to tighten. "And 'twas done recently, with an ax." He shook his head angrily. "Who would have done such a thing?"

Josiah knew his father was only thinking out loud, that he wasn't really asking him. Josiah didn't have to answer . . . except that he knew who it was. Except that he'd tried for too long to do things on his own, and it never worked. Except he had kept things from Papa too many times in the past. Except that his father needed what he knew.

"Papa?" he said.

His father looked up.

"I've seen this kind of work before," Josiah said. "The same people who cut down the widow's cabin did this, I'm sure."

Papa nodded grimly. "And it doesn't take much guessing to figure out who that was, eh?"

Josiah shook his head and waited. His father studied his ruined walkway for a minute, and then he rubbed his hands together.

"I'll need your help to repair this," he said.

"Aye, sir!"

"And it looks as if I'll need your help for a lot more than that in the weeks to come. We two men can work together, eh, even if no one else will?"

In spite of the worried lines in his father's face and the broken wood that lay all around him, Josiah grinned. And he didn't stop grinning for a long time.

✠ ✠ ✠

1. Lt. John Putnam
2. Widow's Cabin
3. Joseph Putnam
4. Sgt. Putnam
5. Capt. Walcott
6. Rev. Parris
7. Meeting House
8. Hutchinsons' House
9. Nathaniel Putnam
10. Israel Porter
11. Dr. Griggs
12. John Porter's Mill
13. John & Elizabeth
     Proctor

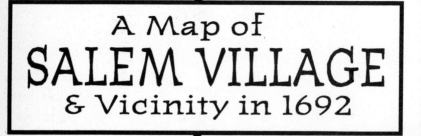

A Map of
SALEM VILLAGE
& Vicinity in 1692

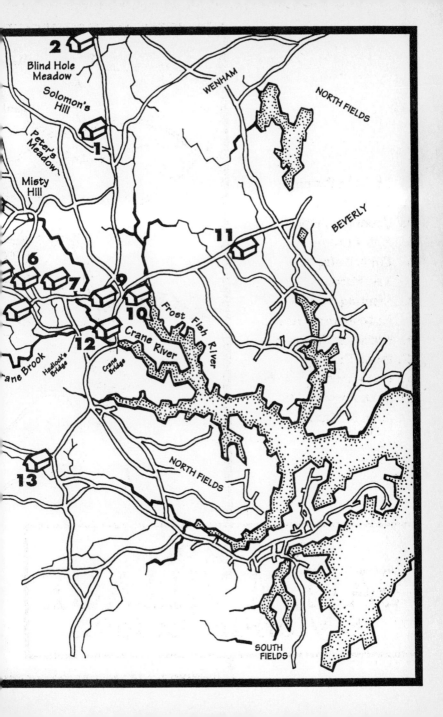

There's More Adventure in the CHRISTIAN HERITAGE SERIES!

The Salem Years, 1689–1691

The Rescue #1

Josiah Hutchinson's sister Hope is terribly ill. Can a stranger—whose presence could destroy the family's relationship with everyone else in Salem Village—save her?

The Stowaway #2

Josiah's dream of becoming a sailor seems within reach. But will the evil schemes of a tough orphan named Simon land Josiah and his sister in a heap of trouble?

The Guardian #3

Josiah has a plan to deal with the wolves threatening the town. Can he carry it out without endangering himself—or Cousin Rebecca, who'll follow him anywhere?

The Accused #4

Robbed by the cruel Putnam brothers, Josiah suddenly finds himself on trial for crimes he didn't commit. Can he convince anyone of his innocence?

The Samaritan #5

Josiah tries to help a starving widow and her daughter. But will his feud with the Putnams wreck everything he's worked for?

The Secret #6

If Papa finds out who Hope's been sneaking away to see, he'll be furious! Josiah knows her secret; should he tell?

The Williamsburg Years, 1780–1781

The Rebel #1

Josiah's great-grandson, Thomas Hutchinson, didn't rob the apothecary shop where he works. So why does he wind up in jail, and will he ever get out?

The Thief #2

Someone's stealing horses in Williamsburg! But is the masked rider Josiah sees the real culprit, and who's behind the mask?

The Burden #3

Thomas knows secrets he can't share. So what can he do when a crazed Walter Clark holds him at gunpoint over a secret he doesn't even know?

The Prisoner #4

As war rages in Williamsburg, Thomas' mentor refuses to fight and is carried off by the Patriots. Now which side will Thomas choose?

The Invasion #5

Word comes that Benedict Arnold and his men are ransacking plantations. Can Thomas and his family protect their homestead—even when it's invaded by British soldiers who take Caroline as a hostage?

The Battle #6

Thomas is surrounded by war! Can he tackle still another fight, taking orders from a woman he doesn't like—and being forbidden to talk about his missing brother?

The Charleston Years, 1860–1861

The Misfit #1

When the crusade to abolish slavery reaches full swing, Thomas Hutchinson's great-grandson Austin is sent to live with slave-holding relatives. How can he ever fit in?

The Ally #2

Austin resolves to teach young slave Henry-James to read, even though it's illegal. If Uncle Drayton finds out, will both boys pay the ultimate price?

The Threat #3

Trouble follows Austin to Uncle Drayton's vacation home. Who are those two men Austin hears scheming against his uncle—and why is a young man tampering with the family stagecoach?

The Trap #4

Austin's slave friend Henry-James beats hired hand Narvel in a wrestling match. Will Narvel get the revenge he seeks by picking fights and trapping Austin in a water well?

The Hostage #5

As north and south move toward civil war, Austin is kidnapped by men determined to stop his father from preaching against slavery. Can he escape?

The Escape #6

With the Civil War breaking out, Austin tries to keep Uncle Drayton from selling Henry-James at the slave auction. Will it work, and can Austin flee South Carolina with the rest of the Hutchinsons before Confederate soldiers find them?

The Chicago Years, 1928–1929

The Trick #1

Rudy and Hildy Helen Hutchinson and their father move to Chicago to live with their rich great-aunt Gussie. Can they survive the bullies they find—not to mention Little Al, a young schemer with hopes of becoming a mobster?

The Chase #2

Rudy and his family face one problem after another—including an accident that sends Rudy to the doctor, and the disappearance of Little Al. But can they make it through a deadly dispute between the mob and the Ku Klux Klan?

The Capture #3

It's Christmastime, but Rudy finds nothing to celebrate. Will his attorney father's defense of a Jewish boy accused of murder—and Hildy Helen's kidnapping—ruin far more than the holiday?

The Stunt #4

Rudy gets in trouble wing-walking on a plane. But can he stay standing as he finds himself in the middle of a battle for racial equality—and Aunt Gussie's dangerous fight for workers' rights?

FOCUS ON THE FAMILY®

Like this book?

Then you'll love *Clubhouse* magazine! It's written for kids just like you, and it's loaded with great stories, interesting articles, puzzles, games, and fun things for you to do. Some issues include posters, too! With your parents' permission, we'll even send you a complimentary copy.

Simply write to Focus on the Family, Colorado Springs, CO 80995 (in Canada, write P.O. 9800, Stn. Terminal, Vancouver, B.C. V6B 4G3) and mention that you saw this offer in the back of this book. Or, call 1-800-A-FAMILY (in Canada, call 1-800-661-9800).

You may also visit our Web site (www.family.org) to learn more about the ministry or find out if there is a Focus on the Family office in your country.

•   •   •

"Adventures in Odyssey" is a fantastic series of books, videos, and radio dramas that's fun for the entire family—parents, too! You'll love the twists and turns found in the novels, as well as the excitement packed into every video. And the 30 albums of radio dramas (available on audiocassette or compact disc) are great to listen to in the car, after dinner . . . even at bedtime! You can hear "Adventures in Odyssey" on the radio, too. Call Focus on the Family for a listing of local stations airing these programs or to request any of the "Adventures in Odyssey" resources. They're also available at Christian bookstores everywhere.

Focus on the Family is an organization that is dedicated to helping you and your family establish lasting, loving relationships with each other and the Lord. It's why we exist! If we can assist you or your family in any way, please feel free to contact us. We'd love to hear from you!